Short Stories

Bite-Size Narratives That Keep You Moving

By Micah William Haar

DORRANCE
PUBLISHING CO
EST. 1920
PITTSBURGH, PENNSYLVANIA 15238

Dorrance Publishing Co
585 Alpha Drive
Suite 103
Pittsburgh, PA 15238
Visit our website at *www.dorrancebookstore.com*

ISBN: 979-8-88812-025-5
EISBN: 979-8-88812-525-0

Allegory

The boy "Start-up" woke up one morning and decried his own work in allegory. "Just-get-by" found him there and they enjoyed lunch. Start-up got tired of the oversimplification of Just-get-by. To this day, Start-up wishes he would have pummeled Just-get-by to within an inch of his life, instead he entertained Just-get-by and a lot of his rhetoric stuck.

Just-get-by eventually left, prodded by Start-up. What Start-up did glean from Just-get-by's horrible verbal schlock was that striving for anything is pointless, a viable theory if not taken in the extreme. Even so, Start-up took his earnings from his writing career, and an immense drive he got from sharpening his wit by the stone of Just-get-by's inanity and plodded on.

With Journey, his companion, Start-up stopped at the village called People and entered a bar in the early evening. There was a beautiful woman tending bar, with whom Start-up locked eyes immediately. Firstly, all the other voices in the bar faded while she was looking into his eyes. He approached the bar, and the tendress named Salva entertained him until dawn.

Sadly, Start-up forgot himself while drinking, eating, and enjoying the juice of companionship with Salva and stopped to exclaim, "Journey, Salva, I must go!" Feeling that his time was not a complete waste in the bar People, he paid his bill and left. Start-up was elated to have partied in the bar refreshing himself and diligently moved on with Journey. He would soon learn that his partying would have a price.

Whilst Salva was sharing her feminine virtue in the bar conversing and feeding Start-up, the forgotten mass in People filled his subconscious with narrative foreign to him. On his way with Journey, these People and their tracts, thoughts, and neuroses distracted Start-up enough to compel him to stop at a dangerous oasis named Suicide. There was one way in, which Start-up paid upon entry. There were two ways out, however, one that was large and friendly, and the other narrow and filthy. In the large and friendly way out, Start-up saw dreams of his family and rest in a little while. The dark narrow filthy way was a little closer, but promised a much easier way beyond its dark filthy exterior (there was talk that it brought glory on the other side). Start-up intended towards the filthy exit, but quickly learned from it shame and figured the large and familiar way led to peace.

As soon as he made it out of the oasis, he was greeted by a man named Cold Water, who instructed him that while he chose wisely in beating Suicide, the path would narrow significantly and asked Start-up if he had enough money to finish. Start-up said yes, but his main asset was his travelling companion, Journey. Cold Water asked him if he knew Journey would abandon him at Rising Tension. Start-up said no. The final word from Cold Water was that Start-up should have a plan to make it through Rising Tension, to carry him through Climax. Start-up answered in the negative but would be grateful to be filled in. Cold Water said his only help was Jesus and bid Start-up know him. Start-up was instructed and thanked Cold Water, returning on his Journey.

Stressland immediately greeted Start-up even before he left the vicinity of Suicide. He asked God, "Why?" This briar patch gave him no rest after that oasis and the instruction of Cold Water. "I can't manage." Soon he learned to live in the thorns and bristles of Stressland and stayed there a year. He learned the ways of Stressland: what is too much hurt, and when to put up with others, and when to ask for help. Start-up considered staying longer in Stressland, but thought it out of touch with this Jesus, whom he met by Cold Water.

"Journey means too much to me yet. I think Stressland will live by itself; it can no longer help me." As soon as Start-up approached the way out of this Briar Stressland, the path narrowed extremely in keeping with the warning of Cold Water. Start-up found unlikely comfort in this, because it bade him only to stay on the path. The lessons of Stressland were hard won, and didn't allow for much creative thinking.

The discipline Start-up learned on the narrow way changed his thinking extraordinarily. He set out in a dreamy way, and began giving himself in Surety to others. He made it quite a way as Surety, however keeping track of everyone who accepted his name would frequently bump him off the narrow way. Returning to his former name, Start-up became necessary to live.

Start-up and Journey continued, following the narrow way more strictly, completely distancing themselves from Surety. Start-up saw rising Tension and remembered Cold Water's warning that Journey would be separated from him there. Start-up asked Journey about this, and she affirmed it, though not maliciously. She would not be going through Rising Tension with him.

They said goodbye as Rising Tension loomed in the distance.

The lessons learned from People. Suicide, Cold Water, and Stressland and everywhere else he and Journey travelled warmed him as he slowly ascended Rising Tension. He felt he would see Journey again, and Jesus would get him through Climax, the pain of which he could not fathom now.

Nor did he need to worry right now. Scenes from his travels taunted and mocked him in something like picture frames tempting him in the periphery of the path Rising Tension, and drained him of his will. Start-up desperately missed Journey, but deep down knew Jesus would get him through Climax.

While the former things taunted him to give up, the intellectual pains faded and Start-up was freed to ponder the physical burden Rising Tension. Here Jesus's Spirit salved his muscles, cured his sicknesses, and swabbed the sweat from his brow.

Start-up was within sight of Climax. Refreshed from prayer, Satan took the opportunity to profit from the confidence of Start-up, and his bolstering.

"You're almost there, boy. Promise me you will credit me when you beat Climax," said Satan.

"But I don't beat this fight; I must endure it," replied Start-up.

"Then worship me now and give in to this hardship. Jesus is Lord."

"Yes he is, but he also strengthens me as a Beautiful Friend!" Suddenly Satan appeared as a Swan and lighted where Start-up had almost a vertical climb to Climax.

"Come, and I will carry you where you desire," Satan said from the Swan. Start-up recognized that it was Satan and with his last living wit he reached over Climax to the top, feeling as though he were dead. A small voice soothed his body, a body that did not believe it could endure even now at the end. After rising, Start-up ventured down the easy slope from Climax, but now more ready as the paths were bright and warm. The toil the climb took showed on the clothes he was left with, which stayed with him now shining as armor a trophy becoming silk and gold gilding all over.

In the distance he saw Journey, a beautiful young woman with whom distance brought together where it had separated them.

Collapse

I thought I was due an afternoon at the bowling alley. Little did I know they would soon be pulling up the glossy lane wood and using it to repair hardwood floors. It didn't seem like much at the time, but since then extant scrap wood and whatever is left at the hardware store or private holds is all the milled wood that is left. The cutting down of live trees for wood has been "determined illegal indeterminately." That was the slogan by the EPA when act 101 became law. Could they sound more sterile?

Who knew society would just quit? It was three years since COVID-19 vaccines did their work. If we would have shown some humility about that, God's miraculous mercy would have spared us the things he had in store for us, what we are dealing with now. Movies and bowling sound like poodle skirts and the soda fountain right now. Can I get a telegraph?

I had an older car and without oil changes and basic maintenance it died quick. Some of the newer models have some kick, but most of the owners are saving them, along with the last fumes of gas left in the tank for emergencies. There are effectively no more cars left. No grocery stores either.

The block I live on, in Milton, Wisconsin has started a grow operation. No trucks to stock the shelves, no workers to commute to work mean food supplies have become very local. We have some precious livestock that might become a sustainable herd for meat. Nearby Crystal Lake is being tapped by a rotating ushering system like at church but with pails of water instead of the church bulletin. Incidentally Church is stronger than ever because it is the only thing to do Sunday, though it is a three-mile hike. I seriously have to learn to ride a horse.

I have been more musical lately. Piano, guitar, voice, all things that don't take electricity which, needless to say is no more as well. Music takes my mind off winter. This will be the first whole winter we have with no gas or electricity. Most of us are building fireplaces with a make-shift outlet in the center of the roof. I have had to build a chimney from the basement so I don't fall through the old plywood floor.

Act 101, outlawing gas and milled wood made living in this world impossible. We stopped throwing bricks left to right across party lines a long time ago however. While government intervention was annoying at first, eventually all our convenience took a collective shit, so we kind of forgot about politics in order to build a world from the ruins of post-modernity.

Realistically, the green-dronies were right about a lot. The worldwide mean temperature warmed by ten degrees Fahrenheit in one year. Here is where the government went all out with Nazi-like pitting of neighbor against neighbor, having us watch each other in order to maximize recycling and energy compliance, hopefully a check that would save us time. The ice caps melted but the shorelines did not recede dangerously as was predicted. The greatest fallout from the warming was the killing of fresh-water life by blue-green algae. We are still dealing with this. This year, two years after smog-producing entities like cars and factories have passed on, the ten-degree dip has become a nine-degree dip. Swimming in the lake might come back soon.

The right denied global warming from the get-go. One year after Act 101, the world leaders sought to come to an agreement about the mass of garbage in the ocean. Right wing politicos all over called this a waste of time and criminal. "It will pass and there are bigger worries," they said. Well, the mass is still floating in its continent shaped burgeoning, largely due to neglect. I do credit rightist groups for decrying the Stalinesque treatment of the working public as our infrastructure collapsed, however, a policing that needn't have happened.

New building was halted, and Act 101 went along way to replenishing our forests, something that was needed to combat CO2 in the vein of cooling our planet. No one really cares about where they live anymore, electricity, heat and getting from one place to another occupying everyone's mind instead. COVID-19 problems seem silly now. The common thought is our isolation, separation, and vaccination came to prepare us for what we are dealing with now.

Even the hardcore anti-environists started to admit to a dichotomy shift when the hard fact of a ten degree rise in mean global temperature started to become evident. Politics became silly, like a fistfight about professional football. Rivers polluted and what was once a priority became what you are eating for dinner. Workers stayed at home, water and food became scarce, and the world, the "connected" world, the "global community" just farted out.

Most of us are beginning to realize the beauty of an agrarian, communal locality where you work for what you eat and wear. Even the hardliners, who to their credit are holding to conveniences like the return of some heat and electricity are caught up in the esprit de corps of this post-convenience world that is starting to look more and more like a snapshot of the nineteenth century west.

The disaster movies had it all wrong. Not alien invasion taking us by surprise, not a New York City inundated by a receding coastline, not zombies from a deadly disease, not nuclear winter; no one figured we would just fart out. COVID cultivated us. We finally started working together and maybe had a taste of what harder people than us had to deal with. It was as if God gave us the manna of convenience every day to test us, but we hoarded it, argued about meat with the Giver and renounced thanksgiving. God then chastised us by keeping us out of the Promised Land saying, "How do you like me now!" Complaining about the ease of the world wasn't the point. It was always about being thankful for exactly what you have.

One half of the population, prior to the shutdown was imbibing, ingesting, and partaking of everything this world had to offer, with little thought as to how their behavior would memoir. The other half spent all their time decrying technology and sitting on their hands, as if inaction would breed change. Our effort and striving ended up failing because no one could agree. Getting angry and indignant about this fueled more laziness and some really talented people lost their way because they no longer felt relevant in a tech-filled world.

It is funny that technology and intellectualism caused the shutdown of modern and postmodern society, yet how much we touted those very things leading up to that selfsame conclusion? We had such a time calling horse-and buggy "simple," yet the combustion engine failed. How these "third-world" countries are now denizens of learning and education, for they have been living without heat and light for centuries! My car is a rusty ornament in my front yard. I will probably never feel the cool of air-conditioning in my home again. What I prized in myself a kind of anti-technology gene has meted out into a computer-sized hole in my intellect where hunting and a propensity to physical labor should always have been.

All the things we took for granted are no longer our entitlement. Some people are coming out of their houses after years of isolation, and these people are now looked at as wise for not having given in to the common ailment of instant gratification. If not for these people, hording old-course television sets, manual drills, and typewriters we would have nothing of the old world to hold as an example. The Amish are seen as visionary, I even have a horse on order even though I have never ridden one.

I grew up with all the conveniences, now I know the names of everyone on my block. I once valued recreation of a sedentary manner, the kind I now spend reading books. People are referring to the "Days of tech." Where we put up with life, a great vigor has captivated many people. We still miss TV and internet, yet what no one misses is that man, that overarching spirit that seemed to have his vision in place of our own. I can tell you the truth, that man is looking over my shoulder right now and telling me I love school, but summer is here and I am not looking back.

Dead Air

It comes from all over. Work, rest, recreation, hobbying, the media, and even sleep hinge on a word I will borrow from radio broadcasting, "dead air." It could be called dead space, dead time, dead love, heck, dead wrong, but the radio version amounts to "no sound being transmitted." In the minute-to-minute business of radio too much dead air can mean ratings, which can mean jobs and careers. People will just tune out if there is no sound coming from their speakers. The story I want to relate is about a young man who has lost all direction. In society's speaker, analogous to his faith he is producing no sound. But like the radio disc jockey or personality, dead air might be detected after the audience has already tuned out.

Joe woke up from sixteen hours of not being awake. He had no obligations. There were his long-term goals, some errands, and some chores that he figured were important, but he didn't have a motivation for. This left him in a bind. The lack of pressure to perform from an external force made him feel uncreative and he dreaded having to confront a day with birds, sky, and sun and not to feel able to enjoy anything. He went back to sleep and stared at the back of his eyelids some more. He got out of bed and found the day still there.

He had things to eat, but they were all boring, so he would fast until he could buy some good rich food later, so that he could eat all his eyes surveyed. He kind of loathed people and their careful eating, who couldn't find the pleasure in eating anything they wanted. After a cigarette, he mulled over doing some push-ups but didn't feel like it so he sat down in front of the TV and kept mulling over whether or not to do some exercise.

He would use stored energy, not working out to plan some craft. He had no good ideas and therefore congratulated himself on being a homebody who could just enjoy being home. After not being able to watch television because he was bored and nappy, he stopped fasting and raided his fridge. He would still binge eat later and complimented himself on using what he had instead of forcibly starving himself before a good meal. Mom would be proud.

Now full yet unsatisfied socially he would throw money at that problem and visit the bar. His favorite was a little corner place where he could gawk at the bartender girl and feel like he was one of the people. He was a much better person than most because he could have one or two and still drive home. He was sure he had a better handle on things, and didn't have to talk to anyone else to prove that. Thoroughly convinced that he could take his little bartender girl home tonight if he wanted, but not saying a word in edgewise to prove it, he ordered an appetizer plate, consumed it entirely and headed home alone. He enjoyed two cigarettes on the drive back.

Thus, fortified by the food, alcohol, and smoke treats, he stopped into a drive-through simply because it was there. He was always chubby but that would never change and this in his mind entitled him to put whatever in his mouth that he wanted. He ate a double cheeseburger he ordered in three bites and didn't waste much time chewing. He congratulated himself again that he didn't chew carefully like other people who couldn't let it all go. He felt sorry for anyone who couldn't do exactly as they wanted at any moment, and blessed himself with another cigarette.

A prayer to Jesus was in order, a furtive wish that he could go on living forever, full and jolly. To Joe, the greatest folly was living in the moment and not pitying oneself moment to moment, basking in the lukewarm pool of hot faith warmed just enough by cold care for the neighbor.

Sunday was different. He intended to go to church very much but didn't, and for this desire unrealized, he gave himself absolute credit. Instead, he would eat much to take his mind off praying and the people he would disappoint by skipping. Another prayer for himself, one of thanking God for feeling superior to his fellow man, while everyone else was slaving to just live like the heathen.

Self-pity was the drug of choice for Joe. It isolated him warmly and left plenty of time to let his hate free without ever confronting anyone or anything. He was lazy, but his problem was blaming a genetic inhibition to stationary entitlement, occurring in approximately one in seven billion people. Feeling alone in the world is normal enough but Joe felt like he was the martyr of loneliness, loving the feeling but doing nothing to sustain it. One day everyone would notice his plight, but he wasn't doing a damn thing about it.

"Such a great faith I have," he would tell himself; the magnanimous, rich, stupendous life he could live but put off for his family, friends and neighbors he could have by doing nothing. Instead, he would live to hold his special place in the afterlife that no one asked him to.

For Joe, it was better by far to intend good and feel secure than to do good and possibly fail. His current stance on church was:

"God can see me all the time, therefore I am always praying, no need for church. A person has to be dumb to even try to please God," that last a position he was keen on, that he was different and set apart from the majority. Most people didn't understand God like Joe, who knew that you could be a spiritual wimp, that you should try to not try, gaining a better position in the resurrection than others who would strive for virtue.

All of this was going on behind this man's eyes in life, always looking at a screen of some sort, hand in a perpetual bag of chips. To set a time to go to bed was "bourgeois" and "classy," so he just smoked and ate grease until his eyelids couldn't stay open anymore, till two and three in the morning.

It was at this point his spirit uttered something, something he couldn't take back but was perhaps the first sincere expression he ever uttered. As his mortal frame from neglect and overindulgence died and rotted around him, not a prayer of his own anymore than one's mind creates a bowel movement, a Source Unseen reached in and pulled out from Joe's soul an acceptable prayer, "Abba, Father!"

That night he slept deep like he hadn't since he was a child.

Gizmo's Errand

The news struck Gizmo like a blow to the head with the garage sledgehammer. The hard drive that contained personal emails, texts, and other sensitive information was hacked as part of a crime against the company that held the machinery that stored the privacy of his own and more than 100,000 other users of the companies data storage capabilities. This man, Gizmo, certainly felt cheated, considering the fact that he earned the nickname pioneering personal computing with a career that spanned back to the 1960s. Gizmo always felt a bubble of protection from technology, because he was in on the ground floor of modern hardware and software and basically anything with a semiconductor. Gizmo was not ageist, but he felt that the whippersnappers who stole his information broke a trust, even though the crime was after a corporation and not him personally.

When he heard the news, coming from various sources, Gizmo nearly became incontinent. The criminals who stole this information didn't do it from a remote computer and internet, there was too much info to retrieve over wire or air. These guys broke in and stole what they wanted. Talking of terabytes of hard drive space, actual servers, maybe a hundred. That and information they downloaded on machines they brought in this cyber-heist was totaling in hundreds of millions of dollars. It was still too soon to tell, and Mack Inc. (the name of the offended company) was being tight-lipped as to whether government sources were compromised. The thieves literally wiped their collective fingertips and walked out.

Gizmo verified all this newsfeed by trying to access his Mack Inc.

account. He logged in, but was quicky cyber-bullied by what appeared to be a virus placed by the criminals or Mack Inc. itself. Either way, Gizmo believed his stuff was gone, as if by cat burglar. He closed down the browser and walked to clear his mind.

All of this angst was shared by the possibly of up to a million users who paid Mack. Inc. a nominal fee to use their hard drive space to store information. Mack Inc. considered itself in the top echelon of discretion and security: people stored with them because they were considered reliable, and wealthy people trusted them with their information. They were the real deal, spending money on lots of overhead where it mattered, boasting a tight, intelligent core of executives whose portfolio was fired in the furnace of programming early on before Windows and certainly before the free public internet, the same executives boasting great education in top schools. They didn't advertise, instead reinvesting profit back into the company, and target-marketing to people who would appreciate this.

All of this was moot. It was not Gizmo's pride, his money, or his faith in technology that flummoxed him when he found his info was stolen. *All of that is recoverable,* thought Gizmo. His investment was bigger, something more than just money. He would go on and on about being cheated by Big Tech (who just should have seen this coming, everyone agreed!), but it wasn't the judgment error in trust either that was frustrating Gizmo. He considered what he had lost to be of greater value than everyone else who was robbed.

The floors and floors of climate-controlled servers, the largest and most elite known to man, basically held money. Stock secrets, social security numbers, emails (illicit and complicit), even government information were considered safe up to the moment Mack Inc. was compromised. The richest and most influential would take Mack Inc. to court, arguing the value of their information. Most would settle for a voucher to store with them in the future that some would spit on, and others would see it through to the rebuilding of their trust, Mack Inc. coming out on top either way.

Gizmo had a more substantial reason to be upset. Gizmo had a dream, a deep one and one that he wasn't lately having at his age. In his dream he was given a sum of atoms and imbued with the ability to construct his very self, body and soul in a perfect copy of himself. Further, he was given the ability to remember when (the exact moment in time), where (his position in respect to), and how (the exact manner) he could put together himself, body and soul, atom by atom. When he awoke, he remained unaffected, but he remembered when, where, and how he built himself, and how he would ensure he would remember. This information, from atom to molecule, molecule to cell, cell to tissue, tissue to organ, organ to system, and organ system to his very self, he turned into binary code and stored this on the vast memory systems of Mack Inc.

The customers who were hacked in the Mack Inc. crime, around a million, on average only used about one percent of their total allotted space prior to the heist. Most liked to talk about the "terabytes" of hard drive they were involved with because it sounded like the latest. Mack Inc. used a large chunk for development purposes. Gambling that a few numbers of a million or so rich people and their "stock secrets," and the government space that was valuable but not large, Mack Inc. turned around the unused portion of these accounts to people like Gizmo who needed all the space and security they could get. The total hard drive space in which Gizmo stored his very self was four terabytes. He did it in a self-described "prophetic frenzy," in which he remembers working, but not getting tired.

Some might ask, "The amount of information in every atom of even a baby would exceed the reach of every cloud storage system on earth, even given all time recorded." While this is true, Gizmo remembered the type and exact placement of every atom, he did not have to record every one. Some organs and organ systems he was able to build like, half an appendix, or remember the DNA only for his bone marrow, and muscle tissue as a whole. The manner of recording was up to him, but only in the original dream was he forced to remember every atom.

The sad part was, no one would be able to read his particular signature but Gizmo. They probably made payday out of the secrets and information of the rich, and probably would hold the government hostage for its contribution to the storage feats of Mack Inc. it stole but all Gizmo was worth after they stole his work would amount to a bunch of crumpled up paper to those who stole it. To him, in his seventies this theft was worth his whole life.

He thought, after dreaming up the way to essentially build himself in "atomic bricks" he could store all the exact information until he could buy an island to place his new self when his original body died. He didn't know fully how this would happen. He assumed he would meet himself, and having built himself transfer mental and nervous energy and ship the new creature to the island. Whether this transfer amounted to an upload of brain juice or a transfer of souls he did not prepare for. Maybe he would die after all the creating and his built self would act like a vessel or '"heaven" for his own soul, or they would lock eyes and he would just die. Either way, Gizmo had to find the men who had his soul.

Having been in the industry long enough, though not criminally, Gizmo could assume that the dives and haunts he associated with internet hacking and that culture would be a good place to start.

He started online, joining discussion threads in conversations that sounded promising.

Tweecker Eacker 317: Did you hear about "The Hack of Mack."

Dozer1234: Yeah and if you didn't do it I'd shut up!

(This one ended up being a dead end)

Mammoth Soda: I hacked Mack!

(Turns out he just liked a lot of pop-drink)

So Gizmo turned to coffee shops in the part of town that was sure to promise at least a lead in the right direction. The name of the restaurant was Clairvoina. Gizmo had been there plenty of times, usually with his laptop to manage his email account. In the good days, when he wasn't reading or on his laptop, he would see people, mostly teenagers and male, who would haunt these coffee shops signaling to each other in between operations on their devices. These were the pickpockets of our time. Back then, Gizmo ranked them in a mental break he never thought would amount to anything. There were phishers, "16 digit easymony," and the ones in there as a rest stop, the big-time hackers. But since these all went down in these types of establishments, Gizmo had to be on his toes.

The man Gizmo noticed stood right out at Gizmo. He had no laptop, only a smartphone, ostensibly perched on top of the table he was seated at to relieve it from being in his pants pocket. Something told Gizmo this man was not here to garner telephone numbers from the cute baristas. He was enjoying his coffee, for one, as if he were sitting at home listening to his own playlist and not the millennial loop that was repeated every half hour, full of Pink and Black Eyed Peas.

That said, his eyes were not dead, like someone trying to be detached, like someone who lost their romantic attachment "really not at the social scene anymore." No, this man sat there as if there were nowhere he would rather be; like it was his job to sit there and listen to another Jason Mraz song and sip his coffee, and he was loving every minute of it. He was sitting there alone. Gizmo checked his ear for a device as he went towards the bathroom.

Apparently, the man in question noticed Gizmo too, as he stuck his foot out trying to trip Gizmo in a way only someone with ulterior motives would notice. Gizmo hopped over the offending appendage. "Ope. Watch your foot, my friend. It's in the Neutral Zone," he quipped

"I'm sorry," the man replied. "I'm too big for this little place." Gizmo saw no visible ear device in the hollow of the man's ear.

"I like this place," Gizmo said when he realized the man was just curious, not trying to start anything and actually showed a little humility at the obvious move.

"Me too," replied the man. Gizmo took his reaction to all of this as a sign the man may be an asset. "My name is Jacob." The man was still a little surprised.

"Harrison, you can call my Harry." Gizmo gave him his real name not the nickname he earned in the tech world.

"What do you know, Jake, can I call you Jake?"

"Sure." Jake looked askance.

"So, Jake, you look to be about thirty years old, am I right?"

"Thirty-two actually," Jake replied, sitting straighter.

"Would it be wrong for me to say we both are not here to sip coffee?" Gizmo inquired pointedly.

"What would give you that idea, Harry?"

"Just a hunch. I'm not a cop, but you look way too happy to be here. Are you waiting for somebody?"

"No," Jake stated simply.

"That's why I approached you. You look like a guy at work, who loves what he is doing." As Gizmo said this, the man's facial affect broke ear-to-ear into a grin, and he started laughing.

"Ha-ha. Actually, I come in here this time every day. I rent the apartment upstairs. I am unemployed."

Gizmo was a tech guy, but not one who did head math in front of a screen while reading programming literature all day long. Soft, people skills were not part of his training, but he earned great points in the personality department by just being decent to others and hearing people out. He still couldn't reckon why Jake tried to trip him, if he was just here to hang out. He tried a shot in the dark.

"I just got four terabytes of information stolen from me." This would disarm Jake while not committing too much. The information could not reveal anything to the uninitiated.

"Sounds crappy." Jake sounded as if he was trying to hold back a ton of stupid with just his good looks. He wasn't mysterious, he was just young.

"May I sit down?" Gizmo was direct as possible because he was going to have to lead this conversation.

"Go ahead, I don't own it."

"Look, Jake, you live upstairs, I am pretty certain you got your head in the right places, so I am going to be upfront with you. I need your help." Gizmo was now committed. He wondered if he should open up about the information that was hacked without sounding insane.

"Harry, I don't know anything about information technology, let alone the level of terabytes in it. Isn't a terabyte like a sextillion of bits or something crazy like that?"

Gizmo was heartened that Jake knew anything beyond tying his shoe at this point. Though between living above a coffee shop and trying to help strangers, Gizmo believed Jake to be a simple heart who might be of help to him.

"Seeing as how you live above a coffee shop, I am sure you are aware of the potential for hacking in an establishment that uses a public Wi-Fi?" Gizmo tried to sound easy, his life in the lurch.

Jake replied, opening up as if relieving a burden, "Totally, man. Even though you have to be given a password by Clairvoina, I am kind of paranoid if I try to order stuff or access my bank account, even from upstairs."

Have you gotten anything stolen?" asked Gizmo, half serious, though still trying to lead the conversation.

"No, but I think that's because I'm way careful." Jake looked down and his gaze dwelled there.

"Can I order you something?" Gizmo inquired, trying his best to keep Jake talking.

"Man, I wonder what it is your asking. I mean, I meet a lot of people here, and the owner has been great, but what is it you want from me? Terabytes, privacy, hacking? What are you after?"

Gizmo had Jake right where he wanted him and in no uncertain terms asked him, "I want to use your apartment to set up surveillance. I think the person who has my info may spend a lot of time on this side of town. What is in the info will be of no concern to you."

"Will you pay me? We've just met and I am not a charity." Jacob was pouring it on thick and Gizmo was not unaware of that.

"Of course. But I will need to see your place first. I, also, am not a charity."

Jake didn't let up. "I think that itself involves a transaction that I will need to be compensated for."

Despite the back and forth, this stand Jacob was making made Gizmo more certain he met the right guy. Gizmo had money. The trust of the right people was invaluable. "I like the way your head is screwed on, Jake. You show me your place, I'll give you a hundred bucks. I only need to step foot through the door to see if it is suitable. You get paid either way."

"One hundred for five seconds? Count me in."

Gizmo was led up one flight of musty hundred-year-old stairwell that went all the way up with no platform. A large ancient door was at the top, opened with a newer key Gizmo noticed as a later add on.

The apartment was probably nicer in its day a century ago. Gizmo made good on his assumption that he could sum up the apartment's suitability to his cause right away. "Here's the hundred I promised, Jake." Gizmo hesitated and withdrew the C-note slightly before handing it over. "Does this entitle me to a better look inside or do you want to draw up the contract right away? From what I see, I could use some time in here above Clairvoina."

"Are you talking crime, here, Harry? I got to know certain things before I open my pad up to a virtual stranger." Jacob still looked pleased, probably because Gizmo paid up.

"OK, Jake. Here's the plan. I want to find ALL my information, terabytes included. As soon as I find the leads, or am satisfied no one downstairs can help me, I'm gone. Give me one week, after which I will pay you $5,000. If I decide I need longer, we can draw something up at that time."

Jake considered this. "What will that mean for my insurance. Illegal equipment? Are you drilling holes in my floor? I do have a landlord."

"No holes. I have some light, very legal equipment, and he's your landlord. Keep him away and if he sees me, I'm gone and you never see me again. Five thousand for one week, Jake, what's the decision?" Gizmo knew he would not be caught. He was still testing Jacob's mettle.

"What is 'light equipment,' exactly?" A good question.

"I have a large, electromagnetic listener, and a tape recorder. It looks like your sixth-grade science fair project. That's it. If the landlord sees me or my equipment, I'm your Uncle Ned showing off his PA gear."

Gizmo didn't come right out and say it, but the listener device he wanted to bring in had the potential to mess with electrical devices within a certain radius all around. He was capable enough for this not to happen. "What's that about an electromagnet?" Jake inquired. "Sounds like more than 'light equipment.'" Jacob really didn't doubt Gizmo, he was holding out for more money, which he wouldn't get.

"You have trusted me this far. Five thousand is a lot for just one week, Jake. I assure you the gear is not illegal." Gizmo stretched the truth a little. The equipment itself was like a gun. Perfectly legal to own, but potentially criminal if misused.

"Why are you using dated equipment like a tape recorder."

"That falls under 'none of your business,' my friend." Gizmo could have said something, but he didn't want Jake hovering over his shoulder. Actually, Gizmo felt he was being too hard on Jake.

"Fine," Jake replied, "although if your spying becomes anything more, I would like to know."

"Jake, I have a feeling this is going to be the easiest five thousand you have ever made. Again, I do have a smartphone, but the listening device is untraceable, unless someone is looking for it specifically. If the boss is looking, who am I?" Gizmo said with a glimmer in his eye.

"Uncle Ned with the PA equipment," Jake answered resignedly. He remained skeptical, which was good because Gizmo was jerking him around a little. But at five thousand for a week? He couldn't turn this down.

Gizmo went home that night confident. He knew the tech world. He knew how workers in tech… heck, he was a worker in tech for half a century. He also knew the guys who worked in this town, the guys who worked and stole in this town, the guys who liked their coffee black, and their baristas twenty-something. Their work happened in places like Clairvoina. Next time he was there it would be listening through Jake's floor.

The next day Gizmo got to Jake's at six o'clock, first thing. He purposely stayed up late, finding that when he had less than eight hours, he was more alert. He hauled his listener, with the help of Jacob. The thing weighed three hundred pounds in a body of about a cubic yard. He placed it on the old oak floor. "Don't scratch my floor, Harry." Gizmo dismissed him with a wave of the hand.

"You're going to have enough to get this place professionally cleaned the way I'm paying you."

Gizmo turned the thing on and it whirred to life. If anyone was scanning the apartment or the coffee shop underneath, they would register an electric field, but one that could easily come from a large energy draw like an oven or electric laundry dryer, not enough to investigate.

Right away he picked up on a voice, a female voice:

"Do you have the stuff?"

"Sure, dear, when can he pick up?"

Gizmo knew the machine was working, that was enough for now. Gizmo turned on the tape recorder for the next line he picked up on. Something about a break-in that he hoped to pour over later.

The only other hard lead that day Gizmo didn't even record. It was so appropriate, he even took notes. The man referred to Mack Inc., and that he was involved in the "Big one." Gizmo was done with surveillance, done with the apartment. Tomorrow he would go into Clairvoina and make a citizen's arrest.

When Gizmo returned home from Jacob's apartment, he was $5,000 in the hole, but what he heard through the floor that was Clairvoina's ceiling made him happier than five thousand Christmases. A distinctive male voice, mentioning specifics about Mack Inc. and being directly involved in the "Big one." Gizmo couldn't have been any luckier if the man signed a written confession. Plus, he said he would be back at Clairvoina tomorrow and an exact time. Tomorrow, Gizmo would find out where his ones and zeroes were.

The witness of the tape-recorded voice of a man who Gizmo strongly believed knew much about the hacking of his hard drive space was enough for Gizmo to take action. He was not a cop. He did not need "probable cause" or a warrant. He sees the man, he confronts him. Even though he had no legal authority, Gizmo felt justified to use force if necessary.

Gizmo was old. He had the dream about constructing each molecule and cell of himself from atom to atom. This was something he felt ready to die for, and he believed it would make him happy. His self-copy would live on for him, and could potentially make a copy of itself, like a mirror of a mirror into infinity. When the plans for all of this were stolen, Gizmo reflected unabated anger more at God than anyone in particular.

He would opine to no end at why his wife died, why his career was over. When he thought he found happiness in his self-copy and it was taken, he couldn't blame Nothing. Now he would do Something. Take control of random crime and make them work to his ends. Take a malevolent deity who was hurting him and fight back.

Gizmo directed his negative thoughts to the next day. He was satisfied he was in control and would forgive God if he got what he wanted. If not, he himself was greater than a Being who claimed to be just.

All of a sudden the alarm rang. He had been staring at the ceiling all night, being angry at what, an invisible force? No matter, he would be extra alert when he went to Clairvoina to search for the voice he heard through Jacob's floor.

Gizmo dressed in a full gray suit, which he looked good in. He was fitted for it only months ago for the funeral of his wife. This is where his angst began and he had the dream that he thought would be his salvation. He thought he did not need the regular afterlife. That is why molecule to cell, cell to tissue, tissue to organ, organ to organ system and then his soul thrown in gave Gizmo the control he needed to reclaim a happiness God was incapable of. Confidence exuded.

Gizmo looked like a mobster in his gray suit, slicked back hair, and his gold class ring he had already fitted for his pinkie, a sign that he was taking control. He ordered a strawberry Danish and a strong black coffee in a to-go cup. Gizmo was not sure the fact he ordered to go was a sign that he doubted his plan, whether or not his man would show. Either way he planned to stay until he was satisfied. If the man fitting the mental image he had heard through Jake's floor didn't show up, he would try another time or another place. Instantly, however that potentiality would not matter.

Through the door walked a man who looked as if he just got hit by lightning. As he walked in, or powered in the little jingle bell hanging from the elbow dampener rang, and the man's head jerked longly and re-flexively backward and he swatted the little bell as if it was his personal alarm clock and he was startled to wake. Gizmo was sure the flannel he was wearing was misbuttoned. It was also obvious the wild hair on his head chose individual directions as a way to their final destination. The man approached the counter. "Can I have a triple-sugar latte?" From that voice, Gizmo derived the sound he heard through the floor with the listener and determined it was his guy. It was as if the speaker wanted to be direct and sane but all of him wanted to be indirect and crazy. That is what Gizmo heard through the floor.

Gizmo made a distracting move by indicating to a random barista as if his order was ready and approached the counter. While no one was paying attention Gizmo grabbed the crazy man by the wrist in a move he learned practicing self-defense over many years. He went up to the man's ear. Now, if you were looking closely it might look like Gizmo was trying to chew an ear off. He was collected despite. "Come with me if you want to leave here intact." The man nodded his head and Gizmo led him out the front door. Gizmo lessened his grip when they got outside. He then grabbed the man by his collar and pressed his back against the bricks of the wall. "What's your name?" Gizmo didn't really care. He just wanted the man as vulnerable as possible to get as much info as he needed.

"Claire," the man stated and under different circumstances Gizmo might have chuckled.

"Were you at Mack Inc. for the big heist?" The man was terrified.

"No, no, yes I mean. I'm small in the game."

"What do you mean. Where is it stored?" Gizmo had his best gangster on.

"You mean the memory?" The man was being elusive. Gizmo upped the ante.

"My car is parked over there. When you take me to what I want, I will let you go. Until then, consider yourself my personal shoeshine boy."

Gizmo was in rare acting form right now. He didn't really hate the man, other than like an objective distaste for crime. He just figured since the man appeared so nervous, it wouldn't help his cause to be namby-pamby.

"I know very little. Just that they weren't prepared for an in-person heist. Most of their security was online." Gizmo continued pressing him into the wall.

"Sounds like you know a great deal. How close are you to this hack."

"If you want to go that far, man, it was more like a miracle."

Gizmo let him go. "We're going to my car. When you make me happy, I let you go."

"It was initially an effort to steal the million or so social security numbers Mack Inc. was paid to store for private and government sources. We had buyers already lined up and stood to make millions." Gizmo had the guy zip-tied to the passenger seat from the back seats and was doing forty-five on a fifty-five outside town. "We didn't have the capacity for terabytes. Then, our geeks happened on this portion of redundant space and it started hacking us!"

"Talk about that. What was on the redundant space.?

"Well, we got cocky. We were as good as paid, and started poking around The Mack a little. These guys are notorious against crime and the whole thing was turning into a duel between our guys and their security. I was in their building, man."

"Are you a geek?" Gizmo asked.

"Man, I know enough. It was my job to break their servers down and take them out." Claire looked like he was in a confessional talking to a priest. "I'm getting scared, man. Where are you taking me."

"Start from the beginning. How did the redundant space hack you?"

"That's how I tell it. The hacks and geeks split with the money items and I was stuck. It was a long weekend and no one showed up for a few days. More like it hacked me."

"What did the redundant space hack exactly?" Gizmo was enthralled. Claire obviously endured trauma. His skin was pale, along with the obvious nervousness there was mucus-like film all over like a fish belly. His eyes were beyond bloodshot, almost bleeding. He sounded like a smoker in his eighties.

Gizmo was increasingly aware of Claire's health, but didn't want to show it until he learned more.

"Man, I must have been at the Mack for the whole weekend, but when I left it was the same day, same time as when I showed up. Barely breathing, though."

"What possibly could have happened, I mean you look like you've been around the bend a few times." His voice was starting to betray a little fatherly concern. Gizmo was no sadist. Claire started to notice this change.

"Hey, man is that you who was holding me there all weekend? It is. I recognize your voice, but more refreshed. You look like that thing's grandfather." Claire was wild-eyed. "Let me outta here, monster!"

"I'm gonna clip the zip-tie, all right. As a show of good faith." Gizmo did so. "Better?"

"That goes miles. But what the hell did you upload into that machine, man? It was like movie-spirity-Ghostbuster goo all over. Like a grown man being born from the womb of a computer. Are you a messenger from another reality or something?"

"You might say that, or you could say your new best friend. One with a paradigm shift. That was my soul you were looking at, Claire. Tell me more."

"Like I said it seemed like a whole weekend in hell, but on the other hand it was like no time had passed. If that was your soul, man, I already had whatever benefit there was in it."

"It wasn't my soul exactly," Gizmo paused. "It was just the repetition of about four terabytes of DNA in binary code. I had a dream that told me exactly where to put each atom."

"A dream you had about making your soul," Claire affirmed.

"Yes, more accurately about building me, one atom at a time." Gizmo was self-assured.

"And you finished this in time to make the evening news? Someone could work a lifetime at that and not make a difference." Gizmo looked down at Claire with fatherly concern, and for a moment everything seemed clear.

"Well, it seemed to take a lifetime, and then no time at all. Kind of like the time you spent with it. Did anything happen besides you suffering my soul?"

"Nothing much. Do you know theology?"

Gizmo was surprised to hear this from a young man in crime. "A little."

"Then you have heard of theodicy. The question of justice. I was simultaneously destroyed by seeing God, or a little of him, and also being forgiven. I will never be the same. Are you going to try and retrieve it?"

"I think I know enough." Gizmo felt the feeling of joy for the first time in a long time.

"What's your name, man? We're kind of in on this together now. What kind of hell did you go through to conceive this plot?"

"Gizmo. I spent a life of toil to create and make money doing it. I earned that nickname, but I alienated my family in the process. This 'soul dream' was supposed to be me recreating a life and the control I squandered. What happened to the dingbat?"

"It kind of self-consumed. Like me seeing its wasted purpose and its refusal to exist. Like it went to hell."

"That's good," said Gizmo. "I wrote it's code to assert my control over my salvation after my wife died. I thought God was singling me out for special suffering and instead of bearing under I misplaced my anger at God, as if I could do anything to him. If I had that control He couldn't make me suffer anymore."

"Looks like He got the last laugh, eh, Gizmo?" Hearing Claire say this, Gizmo knew he was forgiven.

"Looks that way, kid. I'm glad whatever that was is frying a burger for Satan somewhere."

"I'm glad I met you, Gizmo. If for nothing else to get Mack Inc. off my mind."

"Me too. Where can I drop you off?"

Hot walk

A man looked at the front door of the house to which he held the mortgage, looked at his watch and walked away from the door, away from his residence and kept on walking. He flew on the extra time he had. Releasing his life's burden, ascending in spirit, though physically the burden of his routine stuck fast, he pushed through like a bird learning to fly.

Time carried him under its wings as the bird, flying contrary to all known physics he walked in the spirit of self-control as one walking despite his reputation or ability. It must have been miraculous because with all the electro-psychological depression in the man the load was too much for any man to bear. He had too much fight in him for the walk he was about to take, and not enough sense.

His first conviction was to stop and wait until the sun started to go down. God, family, friends, and beloved bosses and advisors with their voices of influence tugging invisibly on his heartstrings: Turn around, you don't have to do this. It was summer and he had no need for sweat or labor, but was determined for something to happen. He didn't exercise, this was no athletic feat. You could say he was trying to burn energy to feel better, but he could have gone to the gym. To take a long walk today may have seemed contrary to logic; he was even silently bemoaning an imminent death. A cry for help would have made more sense, calling 911, or Mother and Father, but he had done these things. If he wanted to walk to a dry, ignoble death, he thought St. Peter would have more pity than a more dishonorable method. Maybe he would get melanoma, as he hadn't even let the sun color his skin in years.

He didn't set out with the knowledge of how much he would hurt himself; he just let wit after wit unfold, to allow his interior ambitions to translate into one footstep after another. A little way ahead was a sign for a church he attended as a child, Faith Lutheran. He relived the relationships made, broken, the potlucks, hymns sung, and his position as son of the pastor. He didn't go to church much anymore, though his heart was still with the Great Commission.

"Go and make disciples." This stymied his better intellect at times of doubt. His growing intellectualism took over at these times, often concealing his Christianity at times when he should be letting his light shine.

A few miles out, while vacillating between darkness and light already early considering how far he was planning on going, his actual ability to withstand the heat was becoming more prominent than his good sense. Fighting this was harder than the walking. The fight to continue won out.

He was on a back country highway, paved but no signs or markings. He desired to take a piece of low corn from a field, but decided that was as good as turning back. He would not wet his lips until his discernment placed a purpose, until he could find his Anchor, or passed out trying.

He was now living and letting his mind dream. Having walked about eight miles with no water he was becoming dehydrated and his brain needed rest. He found that recalling mentally scenes of movies with an underdog story made him perk up and forget about water, until he approached a small town and was recalling scenes from *Rambo*, he thought better to think of something else.

All around him was life: fields, homes, passing cars. In the mind of this man was the prospect of absolutely dry, unpassable desert. He looked right through several opportunities to quit, and the pubs, police station, parks with fountains and puddles here and there were mere distractions. He was prepared to go a hundred miles if he could find the sort of Enlightenment he envisioned could heal him. He had to make his mind forget the pain and this was the important thing.

Some people drink to forget the pain, some people cut themselves.

The man was so reserved in life, on brain medication but not one to advertise. It's hard to say, even in his innermost thoughts whether or not he thought stepping out of his house that day that he would be torturing himself as he was. His body, ill fitted for this kind of strain as it was, was now consuming itself for hydration, having been in the high sun for two hours. His mind was also turning inwards and hallucinating that he was in hell.

The part of his brain that was telling him not to stop kind of latched on to a punishment fantasy and he was literally walking dead. He could no longer ask for help, on a suicide cruise control with the only damper on the accelerator possibly embodied in the Holy Angels. Again, the strides he made were not in miles. This man was not physically trained for walking, especially in this kind of heat. A smoker, he also indulged in whatever he wanted at the dinner table and on the all-holy Screen.

Finally, he shook out some of the delusional thought and thought he had a hold of his mission. This was a cleansing. All the sweat, toxins released, mind cleared and stimulation would make him as good as new. All he had to do was find the road that circled him home. It was too late to turn back, he wouldn't make it. He had driven these backroads often enough, but walking them was a wholly different view not to mention his health.

At this point the man knew he was sinning. He felt like an Old Testament story in which the LORD commanded him to walk until he returned home regardless of his personal safety. He briefly sat down on a rock, and a biker passing looked at him as if to say, "Do you need help?" but he mustered confidence in his mission and smiled saying, "No thank you."

Now three hours from home, he could almost see the road home on the horizon, five, ten miles away. Walking five of those miles, the man decided he had enough, and to take a nap on the parched mat of grass just off the shoulder of the highway. He was not asking for help, or admitting anything, he just decided not to go anymore. A man walked by who was not asking any questions, "Let's go buddy. Let's get you off this road."

In delirium, "Do I know you?"

$\mathcal{P}$ardon

As the man approached the sleepy prairie berg his mind was occupied with arguably the largest emotional weight any man has ever carried. He was looking for sleep, anywhere he could get it. Manny Uuone exited the State Highway in a town that was large enough to have exits in genuine with signs directing the traffic to streets, food, and attractions and to Manny's weary eyes, motels and hotels. The town was not yet big enough to have much of a nightlife, but Manny was tired, and he didn't plan on staying too long in this part of the world, not in his state of mind.

A dance club sounded nice, but he was quite sure he would be out of place, twenty-eight, admittedly part of his state of mind but being over-tired and a stranger in these parts, he would settle for cable TV and a bed.

He veered off the State Highway toward the directional arrow on the sign off the exit ramp that pointed to a the "Way-off Just-off" motel. Manny quickly sized up his situation. Balancing the cost, price versus ac-commodations, and benefits being what he was looking for, namely a good night's sleep. Taking a right to the "Sundown" was obviously the wrong choice, its parking lot full of motorcycles indicating noise, even though it looked possibly nicer. The "Way-off Just-off," was darkly lit and very junky, but the one or two cars parked in a lot built for eighty cars spelled a good night's sleep. Manny needed sleep.

He parked close to the entryway, the car a loaner his dad set up for him when he got out. The hostess on duty was chatty, and Manny let it go because it was late and a bad part of town and he could sympathize with a diminutive woman who was a little pretty. He lessened the blow of her chattiness by engaging her a little, thereby taking the mystery off himself a little. He didn't need a dynamic of any kind between himself and any other person this particular day.

"I was down to the high school today, let me tell you just about got run over in that parking lot, have you been there?"

"I'm not from around here. It's getting to be summer vacation, right?" He led her forward a little.

"Yeah, right!" She was pleased to encounter a mind that was working, unlike most of the clientele she encountered.

Manny laid it all out, gambling his next words would close the dialogue. "I just got out of prison today after serving ten years for murder."

"My daddy's in jail. County lock up." Foiled. He was talking to a ringer. He could see she wanted to talk more than anything.

"Just—do you mind?" He motioned for his room key. "I'm really tired, you know, considering?"

"Here's your key." She looked at Manny with a mixture of awe and admiration. "Ten years for murder? Why'd they let you out?"

"I'd rather not talk about it." He was telling the truth. That very day, he was a number in a bigger number. Today he was free, pardoned by a governor in the same administration that stole ten years of his life. However, institutionalized he was, however angry he was over the system robbing him of ten years, the load he was carrying demanded one more service to mankind. Something he was carrying in his long-term memory was preventing him from moving on.

He told himself during his time in prison, that this "time" wasn't just in the "doing" that he was holding the spot for the man who really killed Stanton Coalminer. He was doing time for someone else until the authorities could find the real killer. As soon as the governor released the pardon that freed Manny and cleared his name, as soon as Manny smelled free air, almost instantly he knew the score wasn't settled. Protesters outside the prison were there to remind Manny he was only lucky, and that a large segment of the population didn't believe he deserved a pardon at all, least of all a reversal of his life sentence.

The hostess smiled and gave Manny his key with a look that said, "I feel your pain." She couldn't but Manny was grateful for the sentiment and more so just to be getting off to bed. A bed, a car, and the freedom to use them, things he didn't ever think he would have again.

The place had a likely odor—stale and old—but Manny appreciated the attempt someone made to vacuum. Even the cheap paintings nailed to the wall to prevent theft charmed him and he told himself, *I've never seen something so beautiful.* He got lost in a knockoff realist number of a pasture and mountains. In his mind that's where he was, promise of more to come, promise that no matter how he was persecuted by lies, he was free and just as even to be in a pasture with mountains. It steeled his reserve to find the real killer of Stanton Coalminer.

It is said ignorance is no excuse for the law. That said even though Manny was in the dark, he did know he wasn't the killer. The evidence put him out of the country when Stanton was killed, evidence that didn't make it to Manny's murder trial. A resourceful private investigator hired by Manny's equally resourceful family found witnesses to Manny's whereabouts, Canada, and documentation that more than proved he wasn't near the murder scene or murder victim when it happened. It was further proven in appeals court that elements who stood to gain by Manny Uuone's being linked to murder concealed evidence relating to two men—Jackie Fursome and Cedric Newbauer—the men protestors sought to protect by pushing Manny as a better suspect.

Either way, Manny was free, but his history being attached to murder and prison would stain his reputation as long as he lived, the wrong people painting his pardon as political meant he would have a hard time with credit and jobs.

Manny's family was wealthy. So much so that in his youth he resented his upbringing and had the reputation as being a "prodigal." He balked at college and chose to live with relatives in Canada. Stanton Coalminer was a hoodlum with whom Manny shared a dump, one so decrepit

Manny bought out and moved to Saskatchewan rather than endure the hovel. Drugs and poverty led to crime and waste, however and months after Manny left Stanton was killed and Manny blamed, even though he hadn't been in-state anywhere near the time of the murder. The cover-up of crucial evidence combined with the testimony of poor but reputable witnesses that placed Manny near Stanton close enough to establish "beyond a reasonable doubt," implicated Manny in the murder. Jackie Fursome and Cedric Neubauer had no motive, and their DNA could be explained away. It was all over now. Manny was pardoned, but his name still in the dirt. What was weighing on his mind was a fourth suspect, a subject that he must pursue or risk never knowing.

Manny found his room, deciphering signs that he wasn't sure helped, he couldn't figure where they were pointing, finally his room 109, and an old-fashioned metal-key lock. Manny had been witness to some of the foulest health hazards in his ten years of lock-up. Feces, gray sheets that he could have sworn were white at some point, and hairs on like a rotation he wasn't sure weren't kept in a catalogue to be inserted into specific inmates' soup for extra dramatic effect. All told, however, and he didn't want to go back to prison, the hotel will always have an aura. Pet dander, after-prom dates, who knows about the carpet? The aura, the life and lives lived under the surface was well published and enough so that a motel would always inspire caution, even to an ex-con.

Manny was in and out of hotels during his youth, his father a diplomat of sorts in business marketing overseas. Even though they were higher class Manny would always remind himself they were not home. Periodically someone else's nail clippings or hair pieces would show up and Manny's youthful brain wanted to complain but a better angel taught him not to worry his already-busy father.

It was during one of these visits that Manny revealed his plans to move into a common apartment with Stanton Coalminer. Manny was eighteen and wanted to try life on his own.

"Maybe just for the summer," he told his dad but Dad was adamant it was a bad move. He trusted his son, however, and agreed the time on his own would be good for him. Mr. Uuone had his own problems. His boss, William "Biz" Drummwald was retiring, the man who was crucial in appointing him to what amounted to a political position, promoting American interests overseas. Mr. Uuone's job was secure, but anytime a person is working with other countries inimical situations are bound to occur.

Manny was aware of his father's plight and, glad to be where he was right now his mind was free to concentrate on his own unfolding drama. As he exited the prison, he heard the cries of the protesters "Put him back in," "Justice in Murder!" As he walked out, a free man, a name seized his memory and he knew his journey was just beginning.

Nigel, a custodian at one of the hotels he would stay at with his dad, snuck popcorn and soda to Manny while his dad was out doing his work, this time in Germany. Nigel, last name unknown, had spent hours with him during their trips to this favorite hotel from as long as he could re-member, until he was eighteen and stopped going on trips with Dad. The name loomed large to Manny as a benevolence but he rarely thought to it, only as a good memory. He was like a good demon, one of those go-to people of whom a person might say, "I'm glad [so-and-so] is walking this earth with me." He had told this Nigel everything, certain of their common plight. "Nigel is working, Manny is away from home," he would tell himself. They would watch big-kid movies together, like *The God-father*, and kids shows like, *Little Bear*, chowing down on popcorn and soda until his dad came back.

Manny didn't even mention Nigel much, the whole affair being as if Nigel was directly working for his dad, like an uncle who came around infrequently and stayed shortly. When he started questioning and placing blame in the weeks after his pardon and before his release, the truth of Nigel's guilt became clear to Manny as the one who framed him. It hurt to have someone so close and familiar betray him like this, even though he was probably just a pawn and the betrayal would have occurred deep in the bowels of the greater gods of intrigue.

Manny was at his wit's end and he chased sleep in his bed, curiously similar in density to the beds he would sleep in on trips with his dad. He imagined Nigel, good-natured yet swarthy, bringing him cold fried chicken at nine in the evening, from a function in the conference room on the base floor of the German hotel at which he claimed to know "no one and everyone." As he recalled these good times, he took a wet towel and wiped the remote belonging to the "Way-off Just-off," a trick he learned from Nigel who claimed "it is the most filthy part of the room," because no one thinks to clean it.

Manny thought back to when he interacted with Nigel, a period of about eight years, beginning when he first started on trips with Dad to shortly before he was incarcerated. He felt that, Facebook not coming into its own until well after he was put behind bars, Nigel was his personal bio Profile, Manny telling him everything including his dating preferences, high school stories, family info, sports, things he cringed at now that he was sure Nigel killed the man he was framed to have murdered.

There was the thought of doubt, "Who can be sure of anything?" especially when he was thinking of tracking down and killing a man who fit into the father spectrum of his life, and Jackie Fursome and Cedric Newbauer were still out there. His case was now unsolved again, and if his dad were not rich and influential, Manny knew he probably wouldn't have received a pardon. He still qualified his burden as the biggest emotional stress ever, however, and therefore it merited a bigger, more nuanced approach than the two obvious stool pigeons. In other words, Manny told himself, he wouldn't feel so awful if there was a simple answer. He mentally doubled down on that prospect: Childhood friend betrays, young adulthood ruined, reputation shot. "I think that qualifies for a medal!" he reflected and assured himself he must clear his name to do the things he wanted in life.

He was no Sherlock. Fursome and Newbauer were darlings of the left, which painted them as poor victims and money from rich patrons covered them like an angel's wing. Even if he regarded himself as skilled in investigation, he felt God must be leading him to Nigel for the very fact that it was an undesirable outcome.

His family was expecting him home today. He had a call planned, when he knew his father would be home and he would tell them he got caught up in red tape and would be staying in the county of his holding until he was cleared for release. This was a half-truth, the "Way-off Just-off" being in the county of his prison of ten years. His lawyer recommended he stay close for a couple of days until his release could be cemented, and the only red tape was the certificate of pardon, which hadn't arrived yet and was largely ceremonial. He would receive it at his parent's address as a decorative keepsake.

Getting the pardon was unlike any joy that could come close in this life to compare. He was aware of the phenomenon of institutionalization, but he would be working with counselors and somehow the justness of his cause precluded him associating with other released inmates who were guilty. It was during this limbo waiting on word from the governor and his release that Manny was struck with guilt over having made friends with a man who would betray him. His innocence, and the emotional burden resulting for being counted guilty by about half the population, made him feel like a victim.

All of this trouble out of his hands stymied his joy and even though he was out, Manny felt trapped by things he couldn't control, not including Nigel. He knew Nigel framed him, and he would sacrifice his membership in the Visible Church to save his soul, he would do anything.

He would have to fly to Germany, where the hotel was that Nigel worked in. He had no money. Manny had no idea the internet could help, and that in the lobby of the "Way-off Just-off," dirtbag, though it was, there was a machine that could probably handle most if not all of the planning. When he was locked up, the internet was barely out of dial-up, so in his mind he would have to hire a travel agent.

Manny got about fifty dollars when he got out. He was supposed to go home, but he felt as though he should take care of Nigel before declaring himself free. After the gas it took to get to the "Way-off Just-off" he had about ten dollars, and decided to hazard contending with the bikers at the adjacent bar for a couple of beers. The justice of his cause would soon shine upon him.

Manny knew there was a God shining on him. He was plagued by his guilt, not driven by it. The moralization of the inmates who really were guilty yet day and night made noise about their innocence lodged itself in Manny's brain and pushed him into this state of blaming other people. Instinctually, and having no money, he felt the best thing he could do was feel out freedom at the bar, have a good night's sleep and Nigel, and the money to find him, would come.

Manny always took the room as he entered someplace new. As a teenager, after ten years in the pen, and now free, twenty-eight years old, Manny liked to act bigger that his five-ten, 190. He wasn't much of a fighter, he just always told himself, "If I don't have the place sized up the moment I walk in, I may as well turn around and walk out." It was his years following his dad around. Many people would let the bodyguards and accolades make them weak, seeming entitled to the praise. Manny took the protection and accolades with him wherever he went, as confidence whether with people or not.

There is one story of when Manny picked a fight with a fringe, Asian Supremacist gang of about twenty, shortly after his first days in. Apparently, and the story varies, Manny started shouting at about ten of these guys, "Don't you talk about my woman like that!" Everyone stopped stone quiet, but Manny wouldn't stop. "You freaks! This is my jail! I eat Chinese food!" Eventually the Asians took it as a point of honor and engaged Manny physically. He actually made it out after a couple of merciful bystanders saved him. Or the time when he was in high school and just able to make it into a dance club when he picked the busiest thoroughfare of foot traffic and stood there like a signpost, just to be a nuisance. Men with the most beautiful partners, ten years his senior walking in herds around this boy of seventeen, trying not to pick a fight with him because they thought Manny was crazy. At this biker bar, Manny was not impressed.

Even though he was wearing the shirt and jeans he had in the prison "Personal Items" locker, placed there when he was eighteen, ten years ago, and everyone looked perfectly murderous in bald heads and biker patches, they seemed distant and complacent to Manny and therefore weak.

Manny located all the exits with a flash of the eye. Prison seemed to have focused his reflexes overall, and he located a seat at the bar close but not cozy to the fifteen bikers at a seating of thirty. He did not want to draw much or any attention to himself, as he was here only to test the waters. Could he pick up any conversation or murmuring about things on the outside? If he was going to Germany, he first had to establish himself here. He did not need that at the end of a gun or in a hospital.

Suddenly something hit the back of his head. Just before he passed out his last waking thought was *I must have slipped as I adjusted the barstool.* Everything was a blur, and he woke up in a hospital bed, his parents hovering over him.

"Are you awake, son?" His mom and dad looked lovingly at him, as if effusive in their love overflowing to him.

"Yeah," Manny slurred. "What happened?

"You had a guardian angel, Manny!" Dad said proudly.

"Doesn't feel like it." Manny felt like about a hundred hangovers.

"I know, son, but it could have been much worse. One of the people who wanted you jailed hired someone to kill you."

"Dad, I think it has to do with that custodian in Germany who always brought me snacks. I told him everything!" Manny felt simultaneously he let Nigel go and got himself into another pickle.

"Son! You're delirious! We know everything! Nigel couldn't harm a fly!" Dad was incredulous, though so elated to see his son everything else faded.

"So, what happened?" Manny was so grateful to be alive, almost more grateful that he was wrong about his childhood friend, but had to flesh his conspiracy theory out a little more for his peace of mind.

"Those two hoodlums, Jackie Fursome and Stanton Coalminer were hired by a nasty political group. They knew it was an election year and chose our family and you to frame, to cast a dark shadow on the progress I have made in business to make their party seem more sympathetic to the plebiscite. 'Nigel'! You just concentrate on getting better and leave the snooping to us!"

"I didn't know you were into politics, Dad!"

"I'm not really. I guess when the money gets involved, things start to go grayscale a little."

"Fair enough, but how did they know I would be at that bar?" said Manny, still groggy.

"Manny!" Dad was almost in tears. "No one knew where to find you, but one of the killers happened to be at the bar where we found you, and by luck or fate, you happened to be wearing your high school baseball jersey. Your last name 'Uuone' was on the back!"

Rory Stockwell

"Stockwell, get over here. I want you to make a trip to Gino and ask him very firmly to sign these papers. Make a copy, and bring me back the originals."

"Sure thing, Boss!" A hurried look proceeded the grabbing of the papers in the lad of thirteen. He hoped his boss wouldn't catch on to the fact that he planned to rush this transaction to get out in plenty of time for the weekend. Rory knew his boss didn't put up with halfhearted work. Even hurrying this small job would be catalogued in his aging boss's whip-smart mind and instantly punished when it was least convenient to Rory.

Rory took a city bus from his home in the suburbs to the Telephone Book Warehouse where he worked. It was his first job, aside from the five dollars he made shoveling neighborhood snow. His last summer before high school, he was glad it was just a summer job, not just because telephone books had become a dinosaur.

Rory started there taking from the tens of thousands of books in the warehouse and loading ten to a hundred of the pulp volumes at a time into the vehicles of private citizens. These independent contractors would then deliver the phonebooks at a quarter a copy. Rory was hired to fill vehicles with phonebooks. After two weeks on the job the boss decided he needed an assistant, and asked Rory's parents if that was OK since technically it was not in his job description. It would mean a raise and a "skilled labor" position, so Mr. and Mrs. Stockwell assented. Rory became a paid intern, but he wasn't sure he wanted the job.

Even with the promotion and pay raise Rory wasn't sure. He enjoyed loading phonebooks, even when that is all he was doing, and when he was promoted, great! He would be thirteen going into freshman year, younger than most and the experience and money derived would work for his resume, which meant his future. Shortly after starting in his new position, however, Rory started to wonder about his boss, Champ Voley.

Champ was a boulder of a man, under five-ten but a solid 200 pounds. He had a keen eye for inequity, usually when justice pointed his way. He prefaced every decision with a nod to some sort of ethic the rules of which he seemed to have forgotten himself, and himself morphed them into a defense of his every move. His keen intellect had become a machine in service to himself, something Rory picked up on because his heart was youthful and sensitive to injustice. Champ Voley was corrupt, but Rory Stockwell's intuition didn't pick up on this until he started noticing discrepancies in the man's dealings around the warehouse. He had knowledge of only wrongdoing. Deeper hubris in the heart of the sons of Adam hadn't trained his boyish ears yet.

The errors started showing up shortly after his promotion. He called them errors so as not to judge Mr. Voley, and would yet jump on a grenade for his leader. He sensed that evil was there, but maybe it hadn't come to a head, or maybe Rory Stockwell was just too decent a person to let on.

Checks with the wrong dates were par for the course, and if brought to light promptly quashed by Champ Voley as "OK." Foreign return addressed, some with pre-fab stickers and names of other companies drew Rory aback, but again not his business. Rory shut off the question in his mind, *Is what I see what I think?*

This was the moment when the instinct of self-preservation hit Rory, when the load of discrepancy became too much to bear. A routine task, taking some papers to Gino, the foreman, and bringing back the originals. Gino was in charge of warehouse traffic, and shipping and receiving. Rory jockeyed papers for Voley, many times already in his short time in the warehouse. He began to think that was all he did there.

Rory couldn't quite get the idea, why Mr. Voley couldn't just walk over himself, but he dutifully performed the football field length walk about three times a day content he was doing his job and glad to have a job. The filter of his mind, the part that analyzes a situation and determines if it is right or wrong, however, always carved out a neat little corner labeled "Your boss is corrupt" which he ignored in the name of honor. Shutting the voice down that told him to stand up for what he knew was right was becoming increasingly difficult.

On a day when Rory was glad there were cell phones, or he would be taking text messages between Voley and Gino, he began noticing a trend. Rory would bring the papers and say, "Hello, Gino, Mr. Voley asked me to bring you these papers."

Gino would answer promptly, "Put 'em right over there on my desk." This same transaction took place three times a day.

Rory Stockwell would report to Mr. Voley who would tell him to take papers to shred in a gigantic paper shredder that could take twenty pages at a time. Rory enjoyed this time in the stockroom because he could let his mind wander and hide there as long as he needed to.

This was a big job for a thirteen-year-old. Not only did he have an eight-hour day, but he had to arrange his own transportation and work five days a week, a full-time job. When the summer was over, he could put "Professional assistant" on his resume.

But it was this paper transfer from Mr. Champ Voley to the mysterious "Gino" that had snared Rory Stockwell into disobedience. He liked the job, he liked the promotion and deliverance from the toilsome monotony of loading phonebooks (which incidentally were growing redundant due to the growing internet), to a better-paying, less physically grueling job with a status increase. Rory Stockwell could not shake the misalignment of the check dates and return addresses, or why he had to walk them over to Gino three times a day.

Mr. Voley's desk was about a hundred yards from the loading dock.

Mr. Voley smoked cigarettes with Gino and his crew outside the loading dock four times a day first thing, during morning and afternoon breaks and after lunch. *Why does he make me take the trip three times a day when he goes there four times a day to smoke cigarettes?* Rory's capacity to look the other way was shrinking rapidly.

The dance continued late into August, Rory Stockwell alternately jockeying papers to Gino from Mr. Voley and shredding papers and hiding in the stockroom. It would seem like his young brain, starving for the oxygen of learning would deteriorate, even die spending an entire summer doing a questionably needed job repeatedly. Rory Stockwell loved his parents, however, and they did not raise a fool. During one of these days Rory decided to ask the questions he would not ask, and to make something of his time.

It occurred to Rory that there was something of a pattern to his perceived malefaction on the part of his boss. For one, Mr. Champ Voley addressed the morning paper trip to another warehouse, with someone else's name. The afternoon bunch of papers was addressed to himself, not at the present warehouse, to what Rory deduced was his personal home, having heard Voley boast about his wealthy neighborhood on many an occasion. The checks came after lunch, once some days and others twice. The dates on the checks alternated between pre-dating one day prior and three days prior. Every time the drop-off occurred exactly the same: "Hello Gino, Mr. Voley asked me to bring you these papers." Rory would start.

"Thanks, kid put 'em over there on my desk," Gino would respond.

The last week of work before school began, and Rory repeated this bit of "Who's on first?" for all but the last time. Something was different, though. Rory was getting short-circuited by Mr. Voley who would cuss at him apparently to let off steam. Gino would flub his line on the paper hand-off like, "Uh-yeah, kid, just put over there somewhere." Gino's forklifters were running into each other, and Gino was sweating unusually profusely. Rory knew his suspicions were coming to light.

He did a cost-benefit analysis: On the one hand, he could quit, but run the risk of being wrong, that no crime was occurring, and it was all in his head. On the other hand, he could stay, and possibly be implicated as part of the crime. Rory decided to finish off his last week.

The Monday of his last week the warehouse was a wreck. Forklifts digging ruts and eddies, Gino screaming for order and Mr. Champ Voley smoking, at his desk which looked like a dump. When Rory arrived, he started to unconsciously throw the butts under his desk and smash them with his bare feet, the little stabbing embers possibly distracting him from the chaos.

"Rory," said Mr. Voley, almost in a trance-like state, "take these papers to Gino."

"Yes, Mr. Voley!" Rory was ready to walk out, but with a smile he remained, wanting to see what would happen.

As he walked the one hundred yards to Gino's desk, he was sure didn't amount to Chef Boyardee in an Italian restaurant, he was almost crushed by a pallet of phone books falling off a forklift (that's Rory's story, but it wasn't that close in reality). Employees arguing everywhere, he dodged men and equipment to find Gino and try to tell him the line for at least some order.

"Hello, Gino, Mr. Voley asked me to give you these papers." Stifling laughter at the absurdity of it all, Rory was sure of criminality yet vied for an answer that didn't matter.

"Put 'em on the desk, alright?" Gino was abrupt, treating Rory like a fly he had to swat away at.

Rory approached Gino's desk. Strewn papers, overflowing ashtrays and voided checks with visible account numbers and routing information. Right then Rory decided to turn off the comedy and be proactive. He was getting out of there. He would approach Mr. Voley and tender his resignation. Rory tossed the papers on Gino's desk and backed out of the loading dock section.

On the hundred yards back to Mr. Champ Voley's desk Rory sized up his situation and thought about what he was going to say. He decided to pose it as an issue somehow and let Voley decide, not in reality but to make his boss feel in charge, and walk out either way.

By this time Mr. Voley was drenched in sweat pouring off him in rivulets, his shirt completely soaked and seeping past his belt into his lap. He was still smoking at his desk, and between Gino and Mr. Voley the "no smoking" signs were rendered impotent. Mr. Voley looked at Rory like a son, though sizing him up and not lovingly. "Get over here, boy and start shredding papers." Rory smelled alcohol on Voley's breath. Champ Voley had been there all weekend attempting to cover up his misdeeds. "Don't ask any questions, Rory, just start shredding."

Rory's brain split down the middle, with righteous indignation at the suggestion that this were his job on one half, and suffocating fear for his reputation on the other. The emotion was ahead of his few years on earth, but with an intensity that basically made his mind up for him. He knew he would have to be firm or he would be swept away with the sinking ship. He knew his parents would be prouder if he handled himself like a gentleman than if he tried to let off steam with cussing and violence.

"Mr. Voley, I am going home now," Rory said methodically like he was talking to a person afflicted with Alzheimer's. "I am not coming back."

Mr. Voley was done, in another world. "Go," he said, with his head in his hands, "leave this place." Champ Voley was in tears.

So Rory Stockwell left, with stories and his sanity intact. He would devour the memories greedily on the bus ride home.

The Chef

A man of great wealth, having completed his education, and not wanting to squander what he learned in academia, decided to be a chef. His desire was not to be a chef in a restaurant, not a sous chef or line cook or any real desire to attain the rank of head chef. No, he loved the science of cooking—to take the hard work and discipline he learned in college and apply it to his skill in cooking for himself to unlock the secrets of ingestion, digestion, and high taste of all kinds.

The man learned to so burn food that it tasted perfect. He learned to over-season also to perfection and to marry different ingredients in such obscene pairs that they tasted like that was exactly where they were meant to be. The man cooked for the Alderman of the city district where he lived. He cooked for the mayor. He cooked for famous people: rock stars, film actors, and athletes. He cooked for the king of a far-off land called Intundia, who called the meal he ate "Mithplescent, (meaning outstanding)!" He cooked seafood with panache. His steaks were super-hot, with little caramelized bits around the edges. He made all kinds of sandwiches, baked and fresh, with lettuce from a garden on his roof. He cooked homestyle (grilled cheese and tomato soup, to start) so that no one would dare say "this is fancy" in the same breath they said, "this is plain."

He started to own so many restaurants that one in a far-off country called Intundia adopted the name "Mithplescent" because the king recommended it to all his friends! He managed to gold-leaf flaky puff pastry so light and delicate only he could do it to perfection and the French masters exclaimed, "c'est impossible!"

The man, now a chef in genuine (despite his aversion to the title) was versed in 50,000 starches, 25,000 proteins and every vegetable in the all-inclusive *Cook Every Vegetable* guide to cooking vegetables! The combined possibilities that all these ingredients produced required an expert in mathematics to figure out just how many dishes the chef was capable of producing. The expert could recite the pi ratio to the thousandth decimal place, but he quit figuring the numerical breadth of the chef's respective dishes after a million.

Finally, after nearly every man, woman and cognizant child knew his name, and his restaurants, cookbooks, and other influences and these had reached nearly every town, city, state, and country in the world, the chef took a break and was ready to enjoy the rest of his labor and retire.

That is until one day, he lost his sense of taste. He could still smell, cook the things he already knew, but as for coming up with anything new, that would require a very refined palate. He tried to cook, and instead of burning food to perfection, he just overcooked it. His seasonings all had their own opinion, and didn't want to work together. His food pairings became like putting east South America and West Africa together on a map: a person could do it, but it wouldn't work in real life. His seafood was tough; his steaks so wonderfully caramelized around the edges became caramel all the way through. People tasted his "new sandwiches" and decided to make their own at home. Prized rooftop gardens were useless because he couldn't taste them to see if they were fresh. Pastry had too much sugar. In the end, despite raving about his old tomato soup, any new home-cooking ventures in public opinion, were best made at home.

The Alderman said his food was stale. The mayor halted construction on the chef's new ventures in his city (he said, "It's not you, it's me."). Rock stars, actors, and athletes alike echoed the same refrain: "We like you, but we think we could do better ourselves." Intundia put a tariff on the chef's food, allowing it to be shipped in at the rate of only a penny per meal. His mathematical boast of cooking millions of meals failed because he could barely put together a carb, a veggie, and a protein on a plate to taste. Every man, woman and child in every city, state and country on earth now knew him no longer as the chef who could cook anything, but the chef who lost his taste.

So the chef, now convinced by this great account against his abilities, gave up cooking for others. He retreated but didn't retire (you may remember a last-ditch attempt for getting rich quick where he tried to sell books about infomercials on an infomercial!), instead working from home, maintaining a persona on social media telling folks he was, "Coping well!" Privately, however, the cook was a voracious learner, consuming books on history and politics, teaching himself music, keeping fit but most importantly skewing his last sensory wit to continue working with nutrition and eating. He still could no longer taste, and had long since given up any ambition to own restaurants or entertain, however, all his learning was aimed with laser-like precision on one thing: the question of taste, which he was lacking. Could he make money as a chef with only his sense of smell?

He went back to the rock stars, the politicians, the princes, and kings he met in far-off lands and other famous people he met when his name was still great. He asked regular folk, people of no account and those who had distinguished themselves though having no real wealth or title. He was well received, because people still remembered his heyday, while not being interested in eating what he had to offer.

He gleaned from all of these different sorts, classes, and types of people what precisely they liked about eating, or what turned their taste-buds on.

A mother from Boise said she loves eating alone, because she could rarely do that. A trucker from the Dakotas mentioned a little diner he went to that always had spotless utensils, which were a rarity in the diners frequented by truckers. The King of Intundia forgave the chef, and told him that he loved to eat food straight from the kitchen, because his advisors and aides were always stressing meaningless details that spoke to their personal stewardship rather than the quality of the meal. Journeymen laborers were hungry: they wanted big steaks. Athletes remembered sitting at home and taking their time and said they craved this during a hectic season. Because they had an intimate connection with producing food at a very basic level, the farmers he talked to liked white table service, and no budget. Believe it or not, chefs and other people in food service craved an all-you can eat buffet, because they were discouraged from eating in the kitchen.

Our chef came to a realization: this scatterplot of tasters had one thing in common, and it wasn't a single thing to do with the taste of food. People wanted to feel good, while they ate. Ingredients didn't matter, beyond a slight nod to cleanliness and value. People wanted an experience, whether that came from quantity, taste, or both. All of his beholding to technique backfired, precisely because he was emphasizing taste, which he lacked, and his fame failed him there. The chef took one more look at the polls and was amazed. People want to feel good eating, simply put. If he wanted to get back into entertaining with food, he would have to start from scratch, so to speak.

Of course, the chef I am writing about was still differently-abled, that is to say he was still handi-capable elsewhere. He still couldn't taste. His sense of smell and environment would have to govern his rise to fame. A large spike in his social rating would be necessary to garner the exposure for this rise.

The famous and the not-so-famous would be important for his new persona, but they were dubious as to whether he could succeed in Food Entertainment without his sense of taste.

Here the chef devised a secret that could make or break him, his dreams of success, and his ability to make money in Food. If he admitted to himself, even secretly that his venture was a fraud he would be found out and he knew he could not make it back from the hole a second failure would put him through.

He carved out an entire lobe of his brain, in his mind in which to place a recipe, the secret he didn't murmur. Everyone, high and low, rich and poor would benefit from it and he would have the fame of his youth. This would not even be uttered, he only allowed the wisp of a thought, and the signature of the taste he once had. He plucked four fruits from the tree of his taste-memory: salt, sweet, bitter, sour. An unmistakable ingredient was assigned to each taste-bud: a grain of salt, a grain of sugar, a bit of coffee-ground, and one drop of lemon. He added a drop of vegetable oil on the side.

He placed each of these on a plate, called it a dish and laid a dry twig on the plate to fill it out. His masterwork was complete. He wouldn't make any further effort on marketing the restaurant. His diminutive meal, his own hospitality prowess and his belief that the experience makes the meal would mean the difference in the place he called "Lite."

To his restaurant raised from his sensory ashes he called the high, the low, the politician, and the student, the bourgeois and the hourly employee. He launched an advertising campaign. To those carrying out his wishes, he stated: "My restaurant is called 'Lite,' and there is virtually no amount to limit what I want to spend promoting it."

There were elephants parading in Death Valley, with handlers who followed in cars covered in "Lite" decals. Macy's Day Parade featured a balloon shaped like the chef. An expert in smartphone apps. was brought in who wrote a program for reservations that young and old lauded as "very accessible." Television and cable were bombarded with thirty-second spots advertising "Lite" strategically located at suppertime to make the viewer think about food. The chef had accumulated a fortune before he lost his taste, and nearly sunk it in this last-ditch effort to regain his fame, and potential great riches.

The day arrived, the opening of his restaurant. Though the chef loved everyone, and Lite was for everyone, he set the flagship location in a wealthier part of town, simply to get an even reaction from a controlled group. He planned to open in more diverse locations down the road.

People showed up, with the press (who were calling him chef out of respect) and the consensus was that he was a national hero, a self-starter beleaguered with a health issue that would have ruined a lesser professional. Here is ticker-tape praise and everyone was anxious to see what would happen.

Chef took the podium he had setup in front of the restaurant and spoke into the public address system he had set up for the occasion. "I will keep my words few, because everyone wants to eat. My meal is the perfect balance between health and indulgence. I serve only one course, and no drink. If you care to join me I now open. Always, 'eating well.'" Raucous applause followed.

The one-course meal was served, and people were pleased with the sparse fare, some having more. Everyone agreed the meal was perfect and hit all the notes on their taste buds. They said it blended well with no filling. To the chef's surprise the next day, there was an article in the "Taste" section of a local newspaper by a food critic who came incognito to opening night. Outraged by this faux pas at first he continued to read the article, which gave him rave reviews. The critic said the ultra-lean meal was packed with flavor despite its diminutive size. A full meal indeed in one bite with your carb, protein, and vegetable all represented. Great presentation, but critics will criticize (he didn't think it needed garnish!). The meal was not overly filling and the option of a second helping didn't stuff, but kind of re-enforced the awesome blend, and overall great time he had at Lite. A perfect score in the chef's eyes!

Indeed a success, but the chef's sense of honesty consumed him. He did not have the stamina to carry out the lie that his meal was nothing, and that people were just believing the hype he created to promote it. He had created a brand, and now he was going to expose it.

He had a well-known newspaper editor from DC hold a press conference. The high, the low, the famous the obscure, everyone who had been there from the early days, through his taste crash, they were all thinking he was going to thank them for the opening of Lite.

He removed his smock and his chef's hat, approached the podium and spoke plainly, "My friends, I meet you under the guise of someone who has earned your trust. You may understand the success of my new restaurant as a function of my great skill and tenacity. I think I have fooled you. My voracious pursuit in becoming a success again has illuminated my product beyond what it is. My skill at creating an atmosphere, my charm, my personality is what you love. Lite is based on the deception that you can eat such a small portion of food and still be satisfied. I have manipulated your minds to believe that you have eaten something substantial because you have had a good time. Possibly if I was younger I could have pulled this off with alcohol and music, but I'm afraid my desire to be rich and get my reputation back as a restauranteur outweighs any virtue I find left in Lite. I apologize, I express my sorrow we will not be pursuing this business anymore."

The fans and reporters were stunned and aghast, realizing the chef had sunk everything into his rebound. The Chef is reported to reside in Chula Vista.

The Party

No one noticed the woman sitting at the party but me. She was unremarkable physically, though her eyes betrayed possibly some Asian heritage. Her light brown hair was pulled back with a baubled rubber band in a bun that sat between the top of her head and the nape of her neck. A worn but clean maroon sweater was ribbed just enough to hide a trim waist. The jeans she was wearing were also worn enough to look present but occupied. She was fairly complected to blend even more, and the nondescript couch she sat on sealed the deal. The only thing to comment on (even the baubles in her hair were subdued) was what looked like a hard whiskey, neat and lots of it in a chunky glass meant for hard alcohol conspicuously gripped by her right hand.

I glanced at her throughout the night, unmoving, possibly one of those "living statues" hired for atmosphere. The host lived in a building that was converted to apartments from a school with high ceilings. I was never quite sure where to find the bathroom or kitchen, but it sure had high ceilings! In those days the house parties were always smoke-filled and everyone was trying to go home with someone. All this conventionality led me to a fascination with the still, sitting woman.

Still thinking she was paid to sit and look "already taken," I approached with caution. No one noticed her or me, no one gathered around, everyone was thinking about themselves and having a good time. Her head, torso, the hand holding the whiskey, even her eyes didn't move. I was satisfied that she was OK health-wise, mainly because no one else seemed to care. I tried to enjoy the party and forget about her, moving more, talking to strangers, basically trying not to look like I was looking at her. If she was with someone, I didn't want to offend. I managed to enjoy the evening, even forgetting about this still, sitting creature periodically and managing to get a little drunk. My inquisitive nature won out and I promised myself to figure the matter out before I headed home.

The night grew on, I met with friends and the hangers-on started to filter out. Soon it was me, the party's host, Steve, and about ten others who must have been wary of leaving too soon. The woman on the couch did not move a hair.

"Did anyone order a statue?" I said lightly, indicating to the woman sitting still on the couch. The attempt at humor did nothing but illicit some shrugs and brief glances, but Steve, the party's host, pulled me aside.

"She's been here all night," Steve whispered to me covering up his mouth.

"I know," I whispered back. "I've been watching her."

"Did you invite her?" he asked.

"I thought you did," I said, taken aback. "You know, like a living statue."

One of the stragglers who'd stayed late after most of the partiers had left, whom I knew by sight but not by name, jumped in, overhearing our little conference. "That's Tina," he assured us. "I didn't invite her, but she is a usual suspect around these soirees, I'm sure."

He was the first to approach her. He cautiously moved closer and playfully waved his free hand in front of her eyes, keeping about a foot from touching her face.

"Was she like this at the other party where you saw her?" I asked.

"No, I mean she wasn't effervescent or outgoing or anything like that, but she was socializing and I even saw her dance a little." As he was talking the guy got really close into her face with about an inch between his eyes and hers.

"She's not dead. Definite light in the bulb happening." He backed away, satisfied by the encounter that his checkup was profitable. The ten partiers left had turned into five, and of those, all were focused on the sitting still woman ostensibly named Tina. Since I had been watching her, I assumed responsibility for my part of the story and decided to stay in case I could help.

"I'm a doctor." One of the five of us left chimed in. "Let me look at her." He took her pulse, and put his ear against her nose and mouth. "There's life! Blood pumping and breath slow, but there." He looked like he had a few, but still cogent. "She is at the basest of vital signs I have ever seen in someone with their eyes open and upright. Like a slug standing still."

"What do you think is wrong with her?" asked Steve.

"I don't know," said the doc. "Is she here with anyone?" No one answered.

"I don't know her, but I have been kind of observing her all night," I offered.

"I saw her come in," said Steve. "She sat down where she is."

"I have been observing her for about two hours," I said. "She looked just like that the whole time."

The only ones who remained were myself, Steve the host, the doctor, the guy who was messing with Tina and his girlfriend. No one was saying anything, so as a responsible personage I spoke up. "Does anyone see a jacket or purse that might belong to her? Where are the jackets being kept?"

The five of us looked around for a moment or two, and the girlfriend of the guy who named Tina first found something. "I'm the only female here and this is not my purse."

Steve looked awash and grabbed the bag. "That's my girlfriend's. She keeps it here as a spare for when she visits. It's kind of expensive."

I spoke again in keeping with my feeling of responsibility. "I think introductions are in order. My name is Paul."

"Good idea," said Steve. "I put on this shindig. I'm Steve."

"You could call me Dr. Zintoff, or Al."

Finally, the guy who named Tina and was messing around with her emerged, "I'm Zack and this is Wanda," apparently his girlfriend.

Dr. Zintoff or Al was the first to offer anything that looked like wisdom. "Look, we're all here either in this together or not. If this girl is going to be a problem, I think we should decide who is going to stay right now. She may have been given a drug and the authorities might become involved. Are we all in?" Everyone nodded in agreement.

Zack looked perturbed. "What do we do now?"

"Should we call the cops or an ambulance?" Wanda offered.

"She doesn't look all that bad," said Steve. "It's my house and I want to have a handle on things before we go making any calls. If anyone has a problem speak now."

"Let's give it an hour," said Dr. Zintoff. "Can we stay an hour?"

"We'll stay," said Zack and Wanda in tandem.

"You in for an hour, Paul?" asked Steve.

"I'm not leaving until we figure this thing out." I didn't know then how or how much this night was going to affect my life if at all, but that would soon change.

We somehow instinctively knew not to touch her, probably for fear that we would be held culpable if the police investigated. We were about five minutes into the hour we allotted as quitting time. Everyone was tired and hungover. Zack was still having fun waving his hand about six inches in front of Tina the motionless woman. "Stop that, Zack!" barked Wanda. "It's not helping!"

"Back off a little, Wanda," retorted Zack. "I'm keeping things light!"

Dr. Zintoff was a little more inebriated than would befit a doctor, but he was managing to take and record her pulse on a sheet of paper he found. "How come he gets to touch her?" said a now obviously hammered Zack.

"If you quit drinking you would realize he is a doctor," demanded Wanda.

"She's right, Zack. This is my house and the only one who gets that close is Al," Steve said out of necessity. He really wanted his house back.

I began helping Dr. Zintoff by writing down Tina's pulse every five minutes, routine stuff I'm told. I found helping the doctor took my mind off Tina, who still hadn't blinked. If something did happen, I would blame myself for being so stoic and merely noticing her early on, without helping or telling anyone what I saw. Just then I noticed something. "Hey, Al, what's that thing in the corner of her eye?" I asked.

Al replied, in a groggy, tired voice, "Looks like sleep. I wouldn't worry." All of us had stopped drinking by now, even Zack.

I was determined. "I don't think so. It looks like a pull-tab on a lottery card."

Zack confirmed the oddity I had pointed out. "It looks out of place. I'm gonna pull it."

Wanda slapped his hand. "Let the doctor take care of it. You'll ruin her."

Dr. Zintoff mused a little with his hand on his mouth and chin like he was studying a rare flower. "In my ten years of studying medicine in genuine, this takes the cake."

"But, Al," I started, "you've got to be over forty! What do you account for after college, med school, and a residency? There's an obvious gap!" Dr. Zintoff looked flattered at what appeared complimentary, and there was a bit of it in my tone. I was trying to get us to focus.

Dr. Zintoff replied, "I actually spent some time in jail, but let's not go there."

"Of course." I said, smiling at my astute observation.

Steve was straightening up and overheard our conversation. "Hey, Paul, what's your story? I know you from work but not much else. Where are you from?" Steve and I both worked in the same office, he a clerk who handled sensitive mail and I the one who created such mail, to make a long story short. He invited me to this party, but we didn't know each other beyond watercooler talk and the lunchroom. I decided to tell some facts of my life without revealing to much of my history. I didn't really know anyone and I thought the point was still helping Tina.

"I was born out West, went to a state college and moved here to Wisconsin for my job and well, that's where I met you, Steve. That's about it. I like it here in Jefferson County!" People seemed to be OK with that.

By this time, it was twenty minutes into the hour we all agreed to wait. "Where are you two from? I've seen you at another party, Zack."

All of a sudden, Steve dove to place himself in between Wanda's hand and the pull-tab-like thing growing from Tina's eye. He was too late. Wanda had pulled the white tab, along with a lens-like membrane off from Tina's face. We were now a half hour into our agreed hour. "It's been half an hour guys," I revealed.

Steve looked perturbed. "I think body parts coming off changes things. I say we all stay until we figure this out. Agreed?" Everyone nodded. "I guess I can't argue with that!"

Dr. Zintoff was already examining Tina closer, Wanda stood stunned with the contact lens thing she had pulled from Tina's eye. She was not looking like she wanted to give it up. Steve, recovering from trying to dive and stop Wanda from pulling at Tina noticed another abnormality. A white ring, pus-like yet bright and sterile-looking, resembling tendon tissue circling Tina's wrist. It was the wrist holding the glass of whiskey.

"Hey, guys, look at this!" He motioned to the ring around Tina's wrist. "What do you think this is?"

"Good call, Steve," I offered. "Hey, Doc, do you think we can take the glass out of her hand?"

The doctor was still examining the lens attached to the pull-tab Wanda pulled off of Tina's eye and looking into the eye she pulled it from. "This is very interesting," the doctor said, almost entranced.

"What are you seeing in there, Doc?" I asked.

"Nothing I can name, but it looks black. Pure black."

Wanda was coming back to reality, from the trauma she endured by purportedly injuring Tina. We assured her she was OK. I started to try and wrest the whiskey glass from the hand of Tina.

The doctor at this point was going mad looking into the abyss that was behind the thing we pulled off of Tina's eye. "None of us can leave," he said as in a mantra, "this changes everything."

Meanwhile Steve and I were making trouble of our own. While I tried to take the glass of whiskey from Tina's hand the ring around her wrist cracked and her entire hand, along with whiskey glass still gripped by it came off in my hand.

Steve grabbed the whole assembly. "Bottoms up!" He said as he shot the large glass of alcohol still being held by Tina's hand. As he did the power cut off. The lights came back on after a moment and everyone's gaze turned to Tina. Steve dropped Tina's hand and the empty glass it held. From where the hand holding the glass of whiskey used to be. I saw something as mysterious as the blackness Dr. Zintoff noticed in Tina's eye socket. It looked like the aura of a magic wand. Dr. Zintoff was right. We were stuck with this problem.

The thing that took the place of Tina's hand after Zack drank the whiskey was both strong and beautiful; hand-like but made of pure spirit, putting all art to shame. Wanda was mesmerized by it. Zack became worried. "Wanda! Don't look too hard!"

"I can't help it. It Is so charming!" Wanda exuded.

I worried in like kind about Dr. Zintoff who was similarly taken in by the darkness in Tina's eye. "What did you see in there?" I asked.

"Darkness, pure darkness," he said.

"Is it dangerous?" I asked, leading his answer a bit because I was kind of anxious.

"Darkness of the purest sort. Like you would want to get lost in it," he moaned.

"Why do you suppose it is not dangerous?" I asked. "You seem scared and Wanda is, like, drugged by it."

"We are like kids who got everything we wanted from Christmas," said the doctor, almost giddy. "I think I have seen the substance of a human soul."

All of us were wondering the same thing. With two body parts now morphed into what amounted to deity, was this night going to be a horror or an adventure novel?

I had come to have a lot of respect for these people who had been strangers before tonight. What happen to us as this night played out finally didn't change that.

"I think the question is not what body part is going to come off next, but when," Dr. Zintoff stated plainly.

"What do you mean?" I asked.

"I mean, I think we should take her clothes off," he chortled, like a nerdy science teacher.

"Like undress her?" Wanda asked with a start.

We all thought both Wanda and the doctor wanted to see more of Tina's soul. We all kind of did but were uncertain of the eternal implication. Were we experiencing an evil, or a good?

"No," replied the doctor, "we cut her clothes off and look for more signs of the white matter that seems to indicate more parts coming off. I think we have to protect Tina and follow this until the end. It's like when you were sick from school and your mother didn't believe you until you were absolutely ill. Then she took you out the day and waited on you hand and foot! If we give her to a hospital now they'll never believe us."

"It's getting to a wee hour," Steve suggested. "How long is this going to take? The party is over!"

"Hey, Steve, we have an eye and a hand. Why don't we do as the doctor says. We are going to want control over this as thoroughly as possible. Hey, and we may never get another chance to see a human soul, right?"

"I guess, but I'm telling you this is my apartment and I don't want anything illegal going down, OK?"

We began to cut her clothes away, all agreeing to leave her underwear on as long as possible. Wanda was peeling her socks off when the apartment shook like heavy thunder and the lights cut out again.

"I can't see. Can you hear me, Zack?" Wanda probed the darkness.

"Here I am, baby." They managed to find each other and embrace, and the lights came back on. Everyone felt around for a moment. Tina was gone. On the couch where she sat there was a note. Steve picked it up and began to read it while we were all still a little disengaged from what just happened.

"I am a messenger of God. You know me as Tina, a name I took while I mingled on earth for a while. All five of you were in the cusp of losing your faith before tonight. Paul, you were hardening your heart against settling down and really starting your life. Zack and Wanda had been going through the motions and not truly loving God first in their relationship. Dr. Albert Zintoff was uninspired and cold to his patients. Steve, you were wasting your life on decadence. By allowing you to see a bit of the divine, all together, and making you feel like a team doing so was the only way to save your faith. Like a camel going through the eye of a needle, God drew you back. Do not worry about that earthly clothing I put on. The intensity of this will fade. Discuss it among yourselves as you must, but cherish God's forgiveness as the biggest takeaway."

Steve dropped the note. No one said anything and we slowly, silently gathered our things and walked out one by one.

The Vet

The teller handed him the fifty, and they both knew it wasn't his. He kept it, said thank-you, knowing it was going to ruin his day. The drive home was twenty minutes long. After his mother died, little things like this stuck in him like a virus. She said the check read two-fifty, even though he earned two hundred. That would be a bank error in his favor, why was it bothering him so much?

He pulled out of the bank drive-through very angry with himself for letting this go. He was not a thief and it was good to have the extra fifty, but there was something about the teller he didn't like. She seemed a little too pleased that she was making his day, as if to say they were friends. He thought, *Am I a charity case in her eyes?*

Lately the only thing his mind could process was the death of his mother, and his job at the factory. This made him feel too single-minded, and then the little annoyances took what was left of his brain space. *What if the teller made a mistake and I get into trouble. I can't afford to drive back there!* He didn't know that the stress of losing his mother made his brain soft, and what used to be rough-going was now disaster, and he longed to feel normal again.

To illustrate he had a short relationship with a young woman that didn't go so well. This seemed to break him up even further and he was retaining the stress of life even more unsuccessfully because of it. They went on one date and he couldn't stop thinking of her. He could hear her voice in his head continually sounding like she was saying "I love you" even though he knew she hadn't expressed this to him.

The man knew he needed help. He smoked some drug he thought was marijuana but later found out was laced with PCP. This is a powerful agent that made him feel indestructible and he had an altercation with police while it was in his system. He had some time where he had to see a probation officer every month, which lasted a year or so, but the drug-laced incident lasted in his mind forever. His record was eventually expunged and he was able to join the Army. When he started getting mad at God for his life, the thoughts and stress and voices started to stick in his mind even more.

He experienced painful "flashbacks" all the way through young adulthood that isolated him, so he started to believe his experience, the life behind his eyes was the only force driving his life. The altercation while on heavy drugs with police was only the first of many flirtations with the law he had as a teen. He ran naked through a pool hall while having a flashback (a flashback made him re-experience the feelings of having the hardest drugs in his system). Back when there were still pay phones in school, he knocked one off that wall as a cry for help. Instead of getting help for his damaged brain, he held the ire of his classmates for destroying a needed communication line for rides home.

He made more trouble for himself than anyone in the world and this puzzled him. He thought about the bank teller again. It was a matter of fifty dollars. Since he got back from serving overseas the angst and stress didn't get better; they got worse. Thoughts that he would be better off killing himself lingered often. He was taking medication and getting the help he needed before he realized he needed it. He wasn't feeling much better for the therapy and medicine, but he was lucky to be among the few who realized this process of recovery from mental illness could take years.

Life wasn't going as he planned. The thought was he would do three years of hard work in the Army and then live the good life. This couldn't have been more an inaccurate prediction and he often felt like he would rather be back in the uniform.

He knew his life's shorter prospect would be a choice between drinking alcohol and smoking cigarettes, which he loved, and the choice of better health. On the one hand he loved the short-term bliss of doing all the bad things that were pleasing him and on the other hand working at a better life. He knew he couldn't have both.

He had a date with a girl this evening that a cousin set up for him. They were going to go to dinner with one another. It didn't occur to him that he had an extra fifty because of the dumb bank teller and was still stewing that she had it out for him.

He worked at a fiberglass manufacturing operation. He could see doing it for a while, but he didn't like the people he worked with. The ventilation was bad and he went home with this thick epoxy chemical in his hair and all over his clothes. More and more his life became the sum total of the relationships in his life, and this didn't used to be the case. People thought he was strong and he was transitioning into a leader, even though he neither thought this was the case, nor was he enjoying the actual benefits of status.

The doorbell rang. It was his date and she was early. He opened the door saying, "Hello, I'm John."

"Hello, my name is Christin." He was impressed by his initial view of things. She was impressed as well, however a bit overcome by the housekeeping she stole a glance at from the limited scope of his front door entryway, with him standing in the way of a better view. John picked up on this, knowing that he should have picked up better around the house. "We could leave right away; my house isn't much to look at." He tried to mask the fact that he knew she wasn't completely pleased by his housekeeping skills.

"Sure. Where are we going to eat?"

John didn't get the feeling she was a burger and fries girl. Actually, fast food would have been a better choice, but he took one look at her Sunday best and knew he should choose more carefully. "What do you like?

"I'm thinking Mongolian Grill," she said this quickly, without seeming to have had it as a stock answer.

"Sound's good. I haven't been there since before the pandemic," John said.

"It's half capacity but I think we can get in," replied Christin.

Right away John started to think he had to manipulate the evening. He didn't like this about himself, but he had to get to sleep and that was more important than having fun. It was like as if his mother was whispering in his ear, "Don't do anything against your honor," even if that meant sacrificing a date. John was in touch with his feelings to a healthy level but balancing being a good boy and having fun was always the backdrop that concealed the actor.

This passive manipulation in wanting to please became more evident as the two arrived at the restaurant. "Where do you want to sit?" asked the hostess.

John caught a cue from an unknown source and belched out, "Near a window."

The lady asked for clarification, "Excuse me?" she said.

Again, he mumbled, "Didn't you hear me?"

Christin, out of an abundance of care, not wanting to insult the restaurant or her date and not wanting for there to be a fight, butted in and said, "Anywhere would be fine, thank you." Right then and there she started to question the likelihood of another date with John.

John would walk out the front door about every five minutes for a smoke before the hostess asked him politely to "move the smoking toward the rear" of the restaurant. John already knew he shouldn't smoke that close to the entryway, where children and possibly more feeble people could be exposed to the deadly smoke. He lacked anything to offer the conversation and he was having a hard time engaging Christin sensually. He was "being himself" to dangerous levels because it wasn't looking like he was going to get a second date. He would prove to be right.

While driving her home, he was enjoying the fact that he was in the driver's seat because of the lack of masculine control he showed with the words and actions he used during the date. He mumbled something like, "Care to see me again?" Christin blushed not from flattery but because she was on the spot.

"I don't think so, John. I liked the meal and everything, but I'm not ready to hold your hand like it seems you need. I'm sorry." He pulled up at her house and they parted with no further words.

Is thick skin more than a fat midsection? John thought so. He didn't show hurt, but felt it keenly enough and deeply even more because he was unhealthy. Things like a bank error and being rejected romantically stung at a level a person cannot always see. An internal death is meant for our good, but if you let more than a few of these go, they get worse and self-harm of many kinds can follow. John resolved to never commit suicide, though it did knock at his door occasionally.

John headed home and parked his car. He had values deeper than issues that had nothing to do with him. Love of country started with love of self and responsibility in how he treated others. He believed that for a man to accept responsibility showed that there is a God. The cigarette that he was now smoking, the morality that caused him to have it in his lungs wasn't up for debate, though.

Cutting corners in life gave John a sense of humor. He paid his bills, made it to work, somehow managed to stay in good hygiene and maintain a social life but his own mind and instinct often eluded him.

He settled down, had some ice cream because Christin wanted to leave before dessert. He went to sleep early; he kept a tight hold on the ingesting of life, and his sleep because of the meds. He would come to terms and be perfect someday, but that day was kept distant in the name of being incremental, or not making too large strides at once.

The hour before bed was always filled with thoughts of family. Some good memories, but he always felt that he was too reliant on them, and that this could ruin his credibility. They always said, "Don't worry," but he wondered at the saliency of this comment. If things like mortgage and car and bills kept getting in the way, would he lose his family's blessing?

After his mother died, the siblings' rivalry calmed down; however, John desired to keep it this way so his job at the factory became very important. He did not want to fight with his family over money.

He had a lot riding on his date with Christin namely stability, security and autonomy from relying on his family for emotional friendship. It was only one date and John looked at it realistically as not a break-up but a new opportunity. He had a warm house, was eating well and plenty of showers!

He kind of hated people who didn't believe and value the same things he did. He wasn't antisocial, but people who put convenience and ease above the common good were last on his prayer list. They were the sort of enemy that didn't die. You will always know where a flesh-and-blood enemy is coming from, but the devil is lurking seen or unseen. His Army exists to make it hard on everyone else and his gain is always power. John didn't have many enemies, but he was convinced that the ones he did have called the shots.

John fell asleep and tried not to think about Christin. He slept good, but even though it was a weekend, he woke up early to keep in touch with his workweek when he had to wake up at six.

The alarm read eight o'clock, two hours later than he intended, but it was deep sleep, the kind of sleep a body needs. John was still young, twenty-nine and almost seven years out of the Army. He was slightly overweight, a smoker and loved the taste of alcohol. For all this slovenliness he considered himself adept and very aware of his nutrition and activity. His prayer was usually, "I know where I have to be and when I get there, I'll start applying myself." He was sure his peers felt the same way. He enjoyed a healthy living, but he concealed from himself the fact that for the lifestyle he wanted he was not behaving the way he should. His social life apart from family was nil and this non-date with Christin proved his skills were just as negatory.

His mind raced and ran away from him sometimes, mostly guilt from his past. Then at other times, he could get so wrapped up in his life, permissible to himself and wrapped up in nothing that he loathed other people entirely. He didn't even want to mention to his family that he was unhappy. He didn't think anyone could help. His work ethic was driving him along with the thought that things would get better. He was starting to realize that this was about all a reasonable person could expect, contentment and suffering through life, which is not a bad attitude, but John was miserable.

The fact was, John kept telling himself he had already hit bottom, and life was looking up from where he was. The Lord had a rebuke in store for him, but John would love him for it. The reason God loved John and would continue to love him is he saw through the external to a seed that could grow, something he had earned only by faith.

Weakness

It started out simply. I was caught in a COVID-19 isolation story not un-like billions of other people around the world. I consider myself to be very realistic, my thoughts transparent and as honest as I can be. I need here to emphasize the sameness of my personal COVID saga for that very reason: my significant and secondary others are used to me as run-of-the-mill and honest and until I started writing this, that was that. A facet of my personal geodesic dome has fallen out however, and the uniqueness of my experience because of this change has left me a different man.

The entire narrative of my story would be drivel if it were not true. All externals are the same as anyone else caught off guard by public health orders, limited travel, and a sense that detaching oneself from others while remaining sterile is of utmost importance. This is because I gradually became used to it like everyone else, and like anyone else it be-came the "new normal" to my circle of family and friends at home and in church.

Until I started writing this down, you could say I was the poster child of what a citizen of this country should be during this pandemic, known to run back to the car to grab a forgotten mask, just to avoid the label of one who would flout the rules for personal convenience! The guy who would say, "Let's just go with the rules until we're all vaccinated and ev-erybody will be all right," not that this is the only valid approach to proper care while physically distancing but to emphasize the fact that I was a guy who would go the extra mile to avoid a misunderstanding or social conceit. I had trained myself to be easygoing, which seemed like tasty whipped crème until I discovered mind reading's bare fruit dish. Yes, while sitting at home and avoiding gatherings, I taught myself to mind read.

As an important caveat, before I report on my findings, the mind reading I am referring to is not to be mistaken for the sanctified office of my Lord Jesus Christ who had the ability of all things and was with and was God at creation. He used his status and abilities to root out hypocrisy in the inner man, a blessed and salvatory instinct! I have concocted a more powerful and selfish strand of personal monologue, somewhere in my inner ear.

I now have full vision of the universe, from the limits of scientific knowledge, namely antimatter, the elusive substance, into the very substance of the building blocks of physics, called the "Strong Force."

In fact, I have an amoeba friend who lives in a little-known section of H_2O in the planet Neptune. I don't know if anyone knows there is life on that planet, but I found out there was water and me and the amoeba hit it right off. He was saying how he and a few trillion of his buddies were thinking of squirming through some safe goop and starting a colony at some other water on another part of Neptune. I encouraged my friend by saying that his ambitions are laudable, but also to warn by saying to watch out for chemicals on his way that could end life on that planet!

Me and my friend, the Strong Force, were chatting the other day (he is in charge of holding the nuclei of all the atoms of the world together). He and I actually tore Space and Time apart for about twenty minutes, or about the time it took us to finish a couple ciabatta sandwiches, two Cokes and some kettle-cooked potato chips! In case you are wondering why you didn't notice, this right now is actually a new space-time—we threw the old one into a Black Hole who said he would wipe it out completely— the gap in time went down with our lunch.

From my recliner I divined a lonely blade of grass at the foothills of Mount Everest. He said his name was Larry. Every time the sun comes up shining down on the mountain, Larry springs to life with a new verve, because he and the mountain are in love. He is sad, though, because their love is not understood, he being small vegetable life. There is hope, however, for Larry knows a tree whose roots reach the bedrock of Mount Everest and this tree has been able to communicate messages between them. Larry and the mountain are communicating but still not as physical as they want to be. I expect great things because they are in love.

I have a great relationship with people and characters of the past. Dwight Eisenhower told me he was wrong. His actual message (which got edited out by staffers) was that we are to have affection and include liberally both the military and industrial complexes in our collective worldview. By the time his address hit the airwaves no one knew what he was talking about anyways, so he just left it alone. Former President Lincoln is doing fine; he visits Mary often and they are hoping she'll get out soon. Napoleon is confused. He is still confined to his island, but he hates to share it with all the visitors since it got turned into a tourist locale.

Besides reading other minds and substances, I like to turn my power inwards at times. I travel along my life's vacillating timeline. I see myself in the future and that self tells me if I can come to terms with my past, we might all have a beer sometime and discover another self! My present self is too lazy and as a consequence not much self-improvement takes place in this exercise.

The occasion to pray is implied in mind reading, and the voluminous, conquering, amazing things I am told to do praying, I am already doing by assuming to know everything. My spiritual life now consists of relying on God to forget that I am not serving him as best I should and hoping that I will eventually be rid of all my wicked desires. Neither counting on God as a chalkboard that gets cleaned daily or counting on myself to get all the answers right is currently working. I think I am in transition.

People have been going to spiritism since the Fall. I actually have met some dead people in my letting go of my brain security. While my dream self was being a bridge between the old world and new horizons (and singing a folk tune!), the only glue in a divided world, and my very self the only thing available in this world able to make everyone love themselves, John Wayne was using my back as a footstool and soaking up retirement. I'm glad I quit smoking.

I translate the vision of future prospect in the realm of love. It is the mouth of a savage deity that I must appease with attention so it will go away and give me enough time to collect spiritual ammunition to fight it away again just to keep me alive. I always lose, however and believe that I am loved despite the apparent!

Dreams are transitory to my mind reading and the mind I read could be said to be substantial, not metaphysical, that is my own not something outside me. To speak of antimatter, it the same as matter just as a negative integer is on the same line as a positive one. Antimatter and the study of it is still largely speculatory and the people who study it are more than clueless. I can say that I had a catch with a ball of antimatter with my nephew in the same breath as a scientist can say that antimatter is the footstool of God. My mind-reading powers are as real as the page I am typing into, and the word-processing program I am using is not even half as Satanic as my great-great grandmother would think it is if she saw me using it!

Staying home isn't so bad, and it doesn't hurt that I learned a new skill, peering into bugs and scaling mountains in my mind's eye. Maybe when the bowling alleys open back up, I can apply my energy into something practical or go to a movie! Maybe my mind will really open up and I will think I am funnier!

Xmas Jake

Many unnamed emotions continually attempted to plague the boy, though calling them unnamed and identifying them as emotions was already two steps ahead of him. Instead of taking a step back and analyzing his problem he accepted it and made it his internal new normal, hauling these worries in the spaces boys do not understand yet, between his subatomic building-blocks that he would learn about in high school.

He got this way every year before Christmas during the break from school, always at the part after school let out and before Presents Day. This time was supposed to be a magical, fun time for kids, but for Mike it always seemed like mandatory fun. This time, with school behind and Christmas Eve looming seemed like something out of his control, so much excitement he interpreted it as negative. Mike wasn't a bad seed, just mature for his age, which is probably why God made him emotionally oriented. He knew he expected too much from the holiday; he just didn't know his part yet. He had a light to share, but he dimmed it to match his mood.

Mike felt lukewarm. Adding spiritual heat here, and cooling his emotions there so that he wouldn't have to grow, which was painful. He would traumatize his ego with internal self-berating, which should be a signal in a normal child to ask for help. He came to be used to the kind of autonomy that a shy quiet kid will experience. He didn't have to accept normal pay from the common emotional bursar. Feeling alone was the job, and self-assurance was the reward. Not sinning actively, but maybe not trying as hard as he should to fit in better. To others he felt abnormal, but within safe limits!

This was a good kid, and high academic psychobabble was occurring to him and his people in kind of a "faith-world." The world and court that Jesus advocates for us and against Satan is not always available to us. He kept Mike's reality just secure enough to save his soul yet remaining hungry for his love. Often times our life-world, the world we are accountable for can seem all too pliable. Mike was far enough in a hole of emotion that the guilt we all feel, which is more real at Christmas, was his to manipulate.

Eventually life would wear him down joylessly, always frustrated; every forward thought and emotional foothold he thought he was making only selling him into self-servitude of a kind that would more and more along this downward spiral sell him into the bondage. A vicious self-destruction that would always feel like freedom was looming but never there. A spiritual mass grave with the world population rotting in it. Would he make it out?

He started to become aware of this fate, looming in the future. There a God-given instinct kicked in to do what Mike could to avoid hell. Aware that pagans and Christians were suspicious of one another and simultaneously fueling their suspicion, the circular wreath common to both faiths. Mike was suspicious because of the wreaths and trees because he saw this as a lack of faith in God. Dates, customs, these things seemed excessive to him. If only he could look deeper and see the practical side, that we have these traditions partly to keep us warm during the coldest part of the year! He actually loved the lights and the carols, but that sensuous feeling kind of drove him even further inward. He couldn't wait for Christmas, and then it was over. It seemed to Mike that the spirit of the age who demands our time often overshadowed the merciful Savior who could command from the manger!

He took a walk in the fresh powder snow, the city lights playing off the individual snowflakes. The boy likened the effect to diamonds. Somehow in comparing this normal winter sight, the boy felt injustice because he had never seen a real diamond, and wondered why he didn't see a star in the city. He felt poetic all of the sudden, kicking the snow in disgust and hurrying home.

On the way home he met a classmate. They discussed a lemonade stand they wanted to build in the summer, and the classmate assured Mike he loved a white Christmas too. He didn't know it yet but friendship would save Mike in the end despite his desire to be aloof. "Maybe there is life on the other side of my eyeballs!"

The Christmas tree was no help. He loved it so much he was afraid of idolatry! In school they made paper-tube Santas. "Maybe Mom would put it up on the tree!" He knew that the tree would come down, and felt like a little bit of him would be on there. Mike wanted to hold on to the seasonal loves but in every Christmas, God was training him to let go.

Little dreams loom big in a child's mind! Each of his siblings carved a world of wonder in his mind, a genetic pecking order demanding obedience until he was married, if he was lucky. He felt guilt again that his loyalties would melt with the snow. He could not accept that everyone felt the same about Christmas. All the symbolism of the season was too much for him and he pictured his morbidity dying to his thanks. To light on a fact that is common and well treated, the possibility of suicide. If Mike did approach this subject, he handled with kid gloves.

His faith-world was secure. Approaching emotion, fate, and inevitability sounded like gobbledygook to Mike, who would do well to realize that God would rather us play with the eternal; the material, our people and our time take care and prayer. It was easier for him to give in to the guilt that his own perception deemed his fault and therefore his problem.

The boy was aware of something called a device. Something that may not look appropriate, like a tooth retainer, but did the trick and was reliable. He was not aware of a physical tool or process that could fix his annual winter devastation; however, his mind was so young in years that he came up with a solution that could cure his prayerlessness. He would call it the Jake.

The schools were all about monitoring the mental health of their students these days, and the boy had to endure a lot of counselling and other classes concerning depression and "danger to self." Though he felt that way sometimes, his mind was really pretty healthy and better for the spread for his age. He needed something to get God's attention so he designed the Jake for the times when he wanted to pray but didn't feel right. Mike had a feeling that his internal rightness with God was the most important thing to being healthy, but he still felt alone and couldn't bring himself to tell anyone.

The Jake would be his go between the faith-world, the world he didn't understand, and the Christmassy feelings he loved so much. Heaven and the punishment of life collided and he called it Jake. Guilt was its prime mover. Somehow, he was supposed to pray but guilt prevented this.

It was a feeling in himself he was trying to invoke; he really didn't know what the Jake was in essence. He had good parents and was baptized, but the nature of prayer made it elusive to him. He had heard it said that prayer is to God, but how can we do anything for the Almighty? Guilt itself, being in this world of death, pain and loneliness is the knowledge of these things and periodically the waste of puberty, graduations, family loss, and marriage must be flushed or remain in the mind.

Mike built the Jake to do all of this for him: don't blame God, don't blame yourself. The boy knew God, obeyed his parents, but was still very shy and had not yet dwelt on every passage of the Bible. Though Church and conscience plead, the ears do not listen. The Jake would do it for him.

The Jake is a delusional projection of a lad who was losing his bearings. Logic would say he needs help. Mike says the Jake is his help. Children who can pray effectively are few and far between, and Christ is the mediator of all. Mike knew all of this in his way but the Jake was very real to him, a way of approaching God, the intermediary, with an intermediary.

This machine was as real to Mike as a heresy is to a heretic. In fact, the very influences that were telling him to be quiet, do what you are told, and accept challenges because you will never be happy were the very wood that he would feed into the Jake to fuel its fire: input bad feelings, output good feelings.

Children understand two things: what is false, and the fact that they do not want to be the agent by which things are made right. They cannot work, and that is why they are children. This disparity is known as dissonance. The Jake allowed the right answer without the guilt or tension that can come from putting off the work of deciding.

The problem with this was it left Mike's brain feeling like it was a blanket of snow in high sun, like the tension was just bouncing off temporarily only to melt his resolve later. He went around thinking of problems relating to feeling terrible and feeding them to the Jake. What was left was like a brainwashing. He had to tweak the Jake to make it transform guilt, and not merely scrub his conscience clear.

Mike wanted to maximize the feeling good capabilities of the Jake. The danger was to have a lot of prayers go into the Jake yet only one outcome—the prayers were answered. Instantly it was impossible to pray to God for anything physical. The Jake was supposed to make him a more effective prayer, and that was supposed to result in peace of consciousness. What it was doing was deflecting bad feelings but doing nothing for the well-being.

Mike decided a paradigm shift was in order. The Christmas Jake cannot make decisions, he would have to make it BE the decision. No one or nothing can make decisions for anyone else. God doesn't want to, parents refuse, and friends can only offer advice. The Jake was deflecting bad feelings and that is good only as a temporary solution. The Jake was intended as a device and that is what it would be. A prayer machine.

The best machines are simple. Merely deflecting bad feelings fails because sometimes they need to be processed before feeding them into prayer. The Jake consisted of two levers (effort and guidance) that worked together to take bad feelings and guilt and bring them to Jesus. Maintenance of the Jake would be up to its owner.

Mike sat under the light of the Christmas tree, his secret self-present, the machine called Jake, completed without worry or harm to its owner. He was not claiming special powers or entitlement, but genuinely at peace that he was ready to give his young life to God and not ashamed. Happy to understand what God wanted from him, he looked up to the precipice of the evergreen and saw it shine like a diamond. In the kitchen he smelled cookies and heard his mother's voice, "Want to lick the spoon?"

Johnny Vinton

It is not enough for someone who holds that he is believed to be something to put up a yellow warning flag; man alone is weak. Man and another can work together, but when he is paired and has ideas about his other, thinking without merit or proof, even to himself, man becomes a danger inconsequentially. Some men left alone go to great power, some to obscurity. Either way the idea we are alone in a room filled with people is not mental illness by itself, nor is spiritual ascetism, something new that fits Johnny Vinton so well.

Johnny gave up on happiness long ago. It seemed too close to femininity so he chose to reject it. His personal ease out-toppled happiness because at its core happiness points up, whereas ease reclines. This mindset lasted as long as his first career, Information Technologies, which he left because he felt his employer was legislating an attitude, which after twenty years a doctrine of contentment sounded suspiciously like enforcing religion.

After a lackluster goodbye, abrupt considering the duration of his tenure, Johnny Vinton took the tools he paid for with his own money and chose some words for his boss that didn't ever make it out of his mouth. Everyone expected Johnny to make a scene, because they weren't unionized and they all took a lot of crap, and had seen Johnny take a lot of crap over the years. He was one of the original crew, yet he could feel his former coworkers quantifying the spot he left vacant.

As he drove home, Johnny realized he had worked eight-hour shifts every day for at least a year and as soon as his body anticipated rest his joints dumped stress-juice that night knocking him out for a solid twelve hours. Rolling out of bed the next day midmorning, Johnny ate about a half a box of Capt'n Crunch, with crunchberries, and dumped heavy cream all over it just because. He then streamed *Pride of the Yankees*, watching it for the second time in its entirety. Throwing on some clothes, he ambled out for a cigarillo he had laid in a drawer a year ago, about the time he started his marathon 365 days without time off. He locked his door and continued smoking, deciding to take a walk downtown. He quickly realized the toll his job had taken as he continued walking the mile or so outside his apartment complex. He barely recognized his face having been in a computer for twenty years.

Still smoking, in shorts and flip-flops, he stewed internally thinking about the unsaid words to his boss and coworkers. He gave them twenty years of his life, yet his attitude wasn't quite up to snuff. Attitude is what makes IT. If he had a smile for every clueless person who should have called customer service but "needed to talk to someone in person," he wouldn't have lasted a year. His attitude kept costs down. His attitude kept his people from getting screwed. He may not have had people skills, but half to three-quarters of the millennial staff only spoke software language. Johnny came in to the game under DOS, honed his skills on early laptops, knew the insides of computers, and how all the components spoke to each other. The current talent knew their game, but Johnny felt lately like he was shepherding a flock of unneeded apps and too-witty fingers.

Walking farther into old Winkler, Wisconsin, he pondered another cigarillo, leaning against a cast iron city garbage spot, squelching the butt dutifully of embers, and sending it down the chute. People didn't put up with tossing butts anymore, neither did Johnny. Even in the days of "free smoking" he always took care of his own mess. He didn't need someone calling him out for the little fiberglass end of a smoke because he was too self-absorbed to pitch it in a can or hold it until he could. Other smokers were like that, but not him. As he raised his eyes from the litter crisis, he saw a shingle, an actual shingle hanging from above a storefront someone had painted with the words "Spiritual Ascetism," and at the bottom, "Inquire within."

More out of boredom than curiosity, and the invite for more that suggested Culligan water and tracts to take home, Johnny Vinton opened the commercial grade double doors and strode into a wormhole that promised something to fill a now eight-hour void that his former job used to fill.

*   *   *   *

As if coming out of the wormhole into the other side of the quasi-spiritual façade was not enough, it became clear that Johnny Vinton, at least in his own hidden narrative, was living absolutely in his own mind, and without the hope of ever escaping it.

This was no waking prison, at least not the one in the medical drama where the patient is physically trapped between complete consciousness and latent awareness. Nor was his confinement an error of a medically induced sleep whereby the patient is inadequately drugged and experiences the pain halfway between sleep and complete awareness. Johnny could speak, could communicate coherent verbiage to the second person, and branched off well into diversifying his resume, having completed a science-fiction screenplay about a Bible counterfeit ring that used content achieved telepathically. He achieved third-place at a competition. The winner got a thousand dollars, Johnny was happy to have the recognition.

Most of what put Johnny here at this crossroads was of his own making. He wasn't depressed. On the contrary he viewed the mentally ill as those who "had something to blame." He was not psychotic; that is someone who is holding emotion as fuel to attack others or oneself, though he did entertain the desire to feign mental illness. He held to a martyr mentality, yet in his dreams and daydreams he saved himself and figured out his problems in thirty minutes, the amount of time it took him to watch a sitcom where things wrapped up nicely in that duration. Johnny actually was terrified of someone knowing him.

The boulder of his lack of care in the waning of his days in IT sat teetering on the precipice of as-it-has-been-going, on the fault-line of life, as feeble as this sounds. People were already predicting disaster for Johnny, his family and friends attempting to package his worry in a religious box, seeming hypocritical, though sincere.

Johnny saw not a wit, not a wish, not a relief of things-how-they-are as worthy of entering the world of "engaged humanity." Any effort to further his earnings or status was fake to him. While performing adequately in his final days of IT, he had adopted the delusion that his death was imminent and that soon he would be "with God," and "away from all of this." Short of suicidal, yet pushing everyone and everything to the periphery as "fluff," only his sacred home of suffering being real. Neither mental illness nor a genius of isolated aloofness was at the heart of the pain Johnny was feeling. He had poured gasoline on his thought prison with his soul inside, and firestarter was tempting.

Having realized this, perhaps at the suggestion of "something new," Johnny felt bold enough to approach the patron, a caricature of a man at six-five, three-fifty with gargantuan hands and a shoulder-to-waist ratio out of comic book history, certainly not in Winkler. The place looked like it was set up for a yoga class, carpet wall-to-wall, mirrored and completely empty.

"Hello, my name is Johnny Vinton. I was enjoying downtown Winkler and I saw your shingle. Based on the sign, I am interested." Johnny winced a bit at his sounding like a job application where none had been offered.

"It is a peculiar person, not a way seeks what I have to offer." The man gave the impression that he was simultaneously pitching and catching his own game, which was oddly refreshing to Johnny.

"What is 'Spiritual Ascetism'?" Johnny cut right to the chase.

"As I stated to anyone it is nothing, but to the right person it is everything."

"How do I know if I am the right person?" Johnny was already intrigued, and tried mildly to mask his interest.

"Tell me if I am right. You have judged that I can sense your attraction to Our endeavor, and you are attempting to hide or alter your facial affectation so as not to betray this fact." The man acted as if he was being interrupted.

"So you have seen all types." Johnny was impressed by the wit in the large man, though still holding back out of self-preservation. Twenty years of disabling cookies and changing people's desktop art gave Johnny scary priority math. He knew a scam.

"Many come seeking health, romantic love or discipline. All this may come but the man right for Our way is enough in being that man."

"Sort of a calling, then?" Johnny was hooked, just still in the water.

"A calling is accurate, though I would equate it to volunteering for the Special Forces before going to bootcamp. Come farther in and let me show you something." The as yet unnamed man led Johnny out of the yoga class-like front into a back room, reeling him in.

"My name is Cresche Vollkern. What I am about to show you will determine your eligibility. Look at this picture." Cresche uncovered a poster of a woman in white slacks who appeared to be dancing. Johnny averted his eyes. He always averted his eyes initially when asked to look at something. It was a bad habit but didn't hurt anything. He then looked at the picture.

"Ha!" exclaimed Cresche Vollkern. "You are now numbered with an extremely small segment of the world population. One in one billion, actually about the population of our reach of the Americas."

"What about the rest of the world?" asked Johnny, not sure of how to take this sensational-sounding rhetoric.

"I believe, Mr. Vinton, there are seven more like you scattered around the earth, and as the population soars above eight billions of human individuals on our globe, that makes eight spiritual ascetics primed for my course of instruction." Mr. Vollkern's face turned cherubic, as if this was his mission statement.

"What exactly is the course of instruction?" Still following but still reticent, Johnny held on to his wits.

"First things first. I did notice you avert your eyes when I uncovered the picture. Do you realize that you did this?"

"It's kind of a habit. When people make it a big deal to show me something, I cringe inside and turn my head. I didn't even know anyone noticed."

"That, my new friend is the quality that I have been looking for. Seven more like you and we have a troupe!"

Why Cresche was making such a big deal Johnny didn't know, saying lightly, "A troupe? Like in a circus?" If there were any social contract between the two, Cresche tore it up right there, though he seemed a little bit like an excited teacher who just got a raise. "What does this bad habit I have had since I was a kid have to do with ascetism?"

"*Spiritual* ascetism, my man! It has everything to do with you. You're the one!"

"Sir, Mr. Vollkern, this logic seems a bit circular. I ask a question, you point to me. I listen, you ask questions. Can you cut to the chase?" Even though he felt he was getting the "treatment" Johnny remained interested, willing to listen.

"It's not strictly about you, Johnny. There are seven more like you, who are ready to work."

"And you just happened on the winning lottery ticket here, in Winkler?" Though jaded by his life's course, Johnny was actually in a state of wonder, kind of like someone being recruited in a cult.

"We have been studying Winkler for a while. Not you particularly but the first we had an idea that he might be here. You are obviously tired. Ponder the weight of what we are offering and come back tomorrow." Johnny felt like he was Dorothy in front of the Emerald Wizard.

"Mr. Vollkern you picked the wrong guy today. Tell me what the deal is or I walk." Johnny was not sorting M and Ms. and Cresche Vollkern knew it.

"What you are looking for is Motive, Mr. Vinton. That I have, yet once I give it to you, you are in my employ and I call the shots. Consider it a verbal contract, agreed?" Cresche stuck out his right hand and Johnny grasped it in his.

"Agreed."

"A worker deserves his wages, and it is not my intention to save cost on my labor pool. I think that what you glean from my instruction is so valuable you will be edified merely by the knowledge, health, and discipline you will receive."

"I thought your way transcended run-of-the-mill philosophy."

"Good thought, my man! But remember, you are the right man, the Way we profess is the plow. To anyone else it is mumbo jumbo." Johnny took stock of his situation having left his job of twenty years and facing unemployment, stumbling onto "Spiritual Ascetism," and now under the spell of Cresche Vollkern. The fact that this whole exchange smacked of a cult did not diminish the fact that he was becoming mesmerized by the logic of it, and he decided that he either put up with the snake oil or avoid getting bit altogether.

"I want to know more." Having had education concerning cults and their preying on lonely young people, he felt he was still in charge of his physical domain, and was yet cautious of what was happening, that it registered on the odd side of the weird spectrum, abnormal on one side and crazy as hell on the other.

"Now, Johnny," Cresche continued as if he gave this pitch before, as if they were on the same page, "the process is simple, and that sets Us apart from the Brainwashing Set—"

Johnny interrupted with, "I hear you using the Collective We a lot," mainly to stay current.

"There are others, and I esteem them highly. But not the eight of you. We are here to cultivate the eight of you."

"Sounds fair." Johnny relaxed a bit.

"Back to the facts. You have heard it said, 'Love yourself', and

'Listen to your heart,' correct?" Now Vollkern the instructor peeks out from behind the clouds!

"Yeah." Johnny was drawn to the line of thinking. "Those phrases work like a Band-Aid until you begin to hemorrhage pints of emotional blood and run home crying."

"Exactly, my man. Psychology failed, so did its cousin therapy. The fight, even mentally is for health. So if you are looking for a medical doctor tell me now so I can show you the door," said Cresche Vollkern.

"I think I will take my chance. Why am I special. What is Spiritual Ascetism?" asked Johnny Vinton.

"People have always wanted to feel good. The Church says, 'Look up!' Society says, 'Look to one another!' but where? The ancients looked to things they could see and touch. I happen to be circumventing all of that. My system looks 'Up,' 'Out,' and 'In,' not to the soul but to an actual part of the human body, which in your case might be one in a billion."

"What is it?" Johnny was full of wonder at what was around the corner.

"Actualities are not priorities. You need a little faith. What you, and seven others like you will experience is the need of nothing. And when even this becomes learned, you will need not even ability. When everyone on earth is assimilated, spiritual ascetism will occur. We will work, 'To God,' and just by existing, our deeds will be deemed perfect. The seed of faith will grow."

"That sounds a bit like heaven," Johnny wondered aloud.

"Ultimately it is. You will be restored to a sinless condition. God's angel will be in tune with your heart's desire." Mr. Vollkern was surprisingly cogent considering his pitch, and the gravity of what he was saying. Johnny picked up on this but tucked it away. Mr. Vollkern showed a breadth of knowledge as one who knew what he was talking about.

"If you could sum this up in a mission statement, what would it be? How do I achieve this potential with my seven fellows?"

"You become influenced, John! You allow me to correct your DNA so that you are perfect, Mind, Body, and Soul." This hit Johnny Vinton like a bag of doorknobs.

"Of course, that sounds good, but it's impossible. What happens after we reverse the devil's touch and Perfect the Universe? Do I belong to you, then?" He was recovering from the initial craze sound of it all.

"No, sir because that would give you the Tree of Life after the Fall. You can't recover from that. Before you submit to the Perfect Influence you agree to work with Us to find the other seven. After they are found, the eight of you will be influenced just by your being; Stasis will occur."

"And what is Stasis?" Asked Johnny.

"The simultaneous death of the old, and springing of new life, a dormancy lasting years."

"And then?" Johnny was like a kid being read a bedtime story.

"Perfection will have arrived, striving ceased, and we will have our Eden." The cherubic look was replaced by fatherly concern in Cresche.

"Sounds like bliss. What exactly do I have to submit to being Influenced?" Johnny asked.

"That is the multimillion-dollar question. You will if you agree submit to a series of tests. These will determine if you have, the 'quality.'"

"What is that?" Johnny's voice cracked.

"Well, once we determine whether you have 'the quality,' you must assert verbally that you possess the ability to be so qualified, and give consent to being associated with that quality, and seven other so qualified, and this all in perpetuity," stated Cresche Vollkern.

"Sounds like an airtight agreement. When can I begin the testing?" Still processing, Johnny was positive. He was looking at himself in déjà vu at this point.

"Step one is complete," said Vollkern. "You are informed. Step two is also complete, you are willing. There is a $100, non-negotiable fee for processing. Cash or credit." The bit of humor was not lost on Johnny.

"I'll have to visit the ATM. Is there one within walking distance? Mr. Vollkern gave Johnny directions. "How long are you open?"

"Long enough for you to make it there and back." With that Johnny took a long walk.

He took his time, and lit another cigarillo, not unaware of the bad habits he would have to avoid. He was not married, not close with his family. Maybe searching for eight friends and making the cosmos perfect was a worthy cause. He waited behind the ATM and thought some more. Besides, being perfect must have its perks, and its downfalls, he guessed. He withdrew the one hundred dollars confidently and strode back to Cresche Vollkern and Spiritual Ascetism.

As he once again pushed the heavy double doors and walked into the carpeted, empty room, there was no sign of Cresche Vollkern. Signs of haste, papers strewn, the picture of the dancing lady laying on the ground. Johnny thought about the day and what he almost got into and hurried off before the authorities came.

Found Money

The fact that I was broke didn't warn me to be extra diligent and to take the penny and save it in a jar, perhaps in the hope to earn a saved penny that might otherwise be despised. I was angry at the penny, and in that emotion angry at God. So I let it sit there on a shelf with knickknacks and souvenirs and mementos, probably placed there in richer times. Maybe I had placed it there trying not to earn or save a sum but with the common thought that "pennies are redundant." Having encountered the penny right now, having no money to speak of, I hated it. If that penny was in my life and worldview, it had a persona and was being tormented by umpteen demons, namely unpaid bills and more to come. I left it on the knickknack shelf as an altar to the unfair God who gave me just enough Mammon to protect, yet again not enough to be carefree.

Loneliness is the accumulation of petty sentimentalities. A person stops being lonely when he realizes that petty sentimentalities are not going to save him, and he should try harder. This penny was one of those accumulations. Now it sat on the shelf as an altar to my weak, poor, forgotten self and his worthless emotions, a mental bookmark to remind me to move on from God, the world, and myself.

Maybe I should have saved it in a jar. I would be one cent in the black, after bills I would have enough to eat until next payday, and this was Hot Pockets and city water. Does anyone think like this? I should stop clicking "watch next episode," at four dollars an episode. I should eat one portion at lunch and save one for dinner. I should have a girlfriend to help me spend my money, but no one can tell me to save a penny.

Life wasn't so bad? Of course, it was. I was living month to month in a measly little pad. The worst part, though was that I had agreed to manage the four-room building, to mow the lawn, take care around the shrubs, and pick up trash that fell out of the communal dumpster. For this, and shoveling in the winter, I lived half rent. The rest was taken care of by a disability check from my time in the service. (I hurt my ankle really bad just before I got out so they would pay me like four hundred a month for the rest of my life). Sounds like I got it taken care of, right? I hadn't mowed the lawn in three weeks and tomorrow it was going to rain all day. The landlord was coming and the place looked bad. I was praying he wouldn't kick me out.

Money worries were taking over my life. I could live in a halfway house. I decided early after college that I would not move back home. It would be easy and free, but there was experience to being bankrupt: milk the government handout until you save enough and then get a job. People respect someone who fought back from poverty more than a lazy man.

This penny, at this moment in my life represented everything wrong about me. Normal people put change in a jar. I really believed I was an economic wimp, that everyone had a correct understanding about money and I didn't. This was true about other things in my life, namely my lack of a love life.

I couldn't find someone, I couldn't find meaningful work, God had forgotten me, I was suffering. I had the crummiest situation too. New in town, out of work, a meaningless sociology degree I got just to take care of military benefits. Eventually even the gratitude of an adoring nation and its glory wane when I couldn't even pay the rent.

Life was one distraction after another, each step distracting from the next, creating a mirage of the ordinary, positivity brainwashing my sense of the genuine. Never truly lighting on a common or absurd thought, my phoniness was perpetually incumbent in a race of one. Friends passing, contentment disfigured, I lived in a spiritual petri dish of unrealized emo-tion, a scientist in the clouds ensuring I did not grow out of the confines of his mundane experiment.

There was yet a purpose in purposelessness. The immature find glory and revenge in this. When I finally matured, I would look back at all my metaphysical gerrymandering of proper social boundary lines as nothing else than the desire for revenge and glory. Youth for youth's sake and this is not to be questioned. Maturity doesn't always equal freedom, and even the old age in body and mind.

A hatred for God, or at least his determinant role, which I perceived was the source of my frustration, lived on much too wavering a line to be a solvent philosophy for a veteran who had parents he claimed to honor. I knew and was taught that "God gives rain to rich and poor alike," and deeply knew Scriptural truths even though my Self wanted to find truth in the tangible. I knew and was taught that pleasure is better a gratification deferred, but that often translated into my immature self: gratify me, delay you.

I was living in a virtual playground, with all the other children in this world fighting for a ball called "Good-feelings. Each one of us felt entitled to the ball; more than that, each of us owned the one ball and claimed to have brought it to the playground.

Another analogy: God kept my heart and soul in a jar, and I called Him daddy. I kept begging for more and more soul treats and He kept giving and giving them without question. This seems true, to the extent that God will give and give to the full. I felt as though, when I felt like this that God suspected me to have gotten sick of his Goodness, and that His continued giving was spoiling me.

About to raise my fist into the air and rant insanely through the little suburban "wasteland" I lived in, hopefully to be taken in somewhere and forget life in captivity, something changed my focus. The gleam of sunlight through a storm cloud (almost surely representing my faith in God) glanced off the penny that was still half shiny despite its age, which I had previously noticed was older. It looked different than most pennies, and as the son of a numismatist, I determined it might be special. Right then

I felt very unworthy of a God who saved a penny from the furnace that could bring his child money into the six figures.